FOURTEEN
SELECTED
SHORT
STORIES
FROM
ACROSS
CONTINENTS

FOURTEEN
SELECTED SHORT STORIES FROM ACROSS CONTINENTS

Vitasta

Published by
Vitasta Publishing Pvt Ltd
2/15, Ansari Road, Daryaganj
New Delhi - 110 002
info@vitastapublishing.com

ISBN: 978-93-90961-98-6

First Edition 2022
Second Reprint 2024
MRP ₹ 350

We gratefully acknowledge Project Gutenberg, Literary Ladies Guide, State University of New York Press, bis.cratercomets.com and The Short Story Project for making this book possible.

Compiled and Edited by Manukriti, Alisha Verma
Typeset & Cover Design by Somesh Kumar Mishra
Printed by Chaman Enterprises, Delhi

The role of a writer is not to say what we can all say, but what we are unable to say.

—Anais Nin

To the writers who said things we could not.

Contents

Publisher's Note

Short stories are like the pieces of a good chocolate bar. Sometimes, we just nibble and enjoy it slowly and on other days, we devour them hungrily. Whichever the choice, the result is always gratifying. Likewise, a good collection of short stories—the most powerful weapons of fiction—can bring immense joy; they are inescapable and absorb their reader until the last word.

Looking at the canon of short stories, one can easily identify a singular narrative, a narrative seeped into our colonized minds. This evokes a self-realization to reject such a closed perspective of the world. Thus, what began as a book for the young and brave audience, led itself into a newer and much clever direction.

While classical short stories are shaped by the society and its strata, there was felt to be a need for intentional gender and locational inclusivity in literature. This was the agenda set for this book. It meant going beyond and above the canon and bringing into limelight a set of short stories to remind us of the vivacious world we live in. Not just the world as is seen by the majority but also by those whose voices have not been heard before.

It meant including Asian, Latin-American, African and other Literature from across the world; giving the reader a glimpse into the myriad shades of emotions felt by those around us and those far, far away; even lived years and centuries before us.

In this collection of short stories, the world can be seen passing through its varied locations as written by fierce women and their male counterparts. From Mansfield's America to Harper's America, Chekov's Russia to Akutagawa's Japan, Wilde's England to Doyle's Baker Street, Maupassant's France to Quiroga's forests of Latin America, Virgina Woolf to Olive Schreiner, it showcases ingenious writers from across the globe as they portray the human condition, looking at life through its love, humour, anxiety, playfulness but most importantly, honesty.

These stories encapsulate moments in time we sensibly see but forget to look back into. With this collection, we intend to make time stop and let ourselves breathe in the wildness that transforms the giant, powerful world into a tiny place of our imagination.

O Henry, USA

Pseudonym of William Sydney Porter
(September 11, 1862 – June 5, 1910)

O Henry, the great American short writer, is known for his surprise endings and believed in romanticising the mundane things, particularly the lives of common people in New York City.

O Henry wandered across different paths and professions before becoming a short story writer. He struggled for a successful career venture amid bankruptcy and his wife's ill health, so he continuously moved across states and even served time in prison. He had a liking for classical literature, so he pursued writing as a hobby. In prison, he decided to write to make money and support his daughter, Margaret. His adventurous tales sparked magazine readers' attention in the southwest US and Central America. Thus, when he emerged from prison, William S Porter had become O Henry, an acclaimed writer.

O Henry passed away in 1910. His vast legacy surmounts countless foreign translations and adaptations across art forms that attest to his universal relevance and appeal. His other works include *Cabbages and Kings* (1904), *The Four Million* (1906) and *The Trimmed Lamp* (1907). Today, The O Henry Prize is an award established in his honour to commemorate his contribution to literature and celebrates a writer annually for their outstanding short stories.

Transients in Arcadia

There is a hotel on Broadway that has escaped discovery by the summer-resort promoters. It is deep and wide and cool. Its rooms are finished in dark oak of a low temperature. Home-made breezes and deep-green shrubbery give it the delights without the inconveniences of the Adirondacks.* One can mount its broad staircases or glide dreamily upward in its aerial elevators, attended by guides in brass buttons, with a serene joy that Alpine climbers have never attained. There is a chef in its kitchen who will prepare for you brook trout better than the White Mountains ever served, sea food that would turn Old Point Comfort—'by Gad, sah!'—green with envy, and Maine venison that would melt the official heart of a game warden.

A few have found out this oasis in the July desert of Manhattan. During that month you will see the hotel's reduced array of guests scattered luxuriously about in the cool twilight of—its lofty dining-room, gazing at one another across the snowy waste of unoccupied tables, silently congratulatory.

Superfluous, watchful, pneumatically moving waiters hover near, supplying every want before it is expressed. The temperature is perpetual April. The ceiling is painted in water colors to counterfeit a summer sky across which delicate clouds drift and do not vanish as those of nature do to our regret.

The pleasing, distant roar of Broadway is transformed in the imagination of the happy guests to the noise of a waterfall filling the woods with its restful sound. At every strange footstep the guests turn an anxious ear, fearful lest their retreat be discovered and invaded by the restless pleasure-seekers who are forever hounding nature to her deepest lairs.

Thus in the depopulated caravansary* the little band of connoisseurs jealously bide themselves during the heated season, enjoying to the uttermost the delights of mountain and seashore that art and skill have gathered and served to them.

In this July came to the hotel one whose card that she sent to the clerk for her name to be registered read 'Mme Heloise D'Arcy Beaumont.'

Madame Beaumont was a guest such as the

Hotel Lotus loved. She possessed the fine air of the elite, tempered and sweetened by a cordial graciousness that made the hotel employees her slaves. Bell-boys fought for the honor of answering her ring; the clerks, but for the question of ownership, would have deeded to her the hotel and its contents; the other guests regarded her as the final touch of feminine exclusiveness and beauty that rendered the entourage perfect.

This super-excellent guest rarely left the hotel. Her habits were consonant with the customs of the discriminating patrons of the Hotel Lotus. To enjoy that delectable hostelry, one must forego the city as though it were leagues away. By night a brief excursion to the nearby roofs is in order; but during the torrid day, one remains in the umbrageous* fastnesses of the Lotus as a trout hangs poised in the pellucid* sanctuaries of his favorite pool.

Though alone in the Hotel Lotus, Madame Beaumont preserved the state of a queen whose loneliness was of position only. She breakfasted at ten, a cool, sweet, leisurely, delicate being who glowed softly in the dimness like a jasmine flower in the dusk.

But at dinner was Madame's glory at its height. She wore a gown as beautiful and immaterial as the mist from an unseen cataract in a mountain gorge. The nomenclature of this gown is beyond the guess of the scribe. Always pale-red roses reposed against its lace-garnished front. It was a gown that the head-waiter viewed with respect and met at the door. You thought of Paris when you saw it, and maybe of mysterious countesses, and certainly of Versailles and rapiers* and Mrs Fiske and *rouge-et-noir*.* There was an untraceable rumor in the Hotel Lotus that Madame was a cosmopolite, and that she was pulling with her slender white bands certain strings between the nations in the favor of Russia. Being a citizeness of the world's smoothest roads it was small wonder that she was quick to recognize in the refined purlieus* of the Hotel Lotus the most desirable spot in America for a restful sojourn during the heat of midsummer.

On the third day of Madame Beaumont's residence in the hotel a young man entered and registered himself as a guest. His clothing—to speak of his points in approved order—was quietly in the mode; his features good and regular; his expression that of a poised and sophisticated man of the world. He informed the clerk that he would remain three or four days, inquired concerning the sailing of European steamships, and sank into the blissful inanition* of the nonpareil* hotel with the contented air of a traveller in his favorite inn.

The young man—not to question the veracity of the register—was Harold Farrington. He drifted into the exclusive and calm current of life in the Lotus so tactfully and silently that not a ripple alarmed his fellow-seekers after rest. He ate in the Lotus and of its patronym,* and was lulled into blissful peace with the other fortunate mariners. In one day he acquired his table and his waiter and the fear lest the panting chasers after repose that kept Broadway warm should pounce upon and destroy this contiguous but covert haven.

After dinner on the next day after the arrival of Harold Farrington Madame Beaumont dropped her handkerchief in passing out. Mr Farrington recovered and returned it without the effusiveness of a seeker after acquaintance.

Perhaps there was a mystic freemasonry* between the discriminating guests of the Lotus. Perhaps they were drawn one to another by the fact of their common good fortune in discovering the acme* of summer resorts in a Broadway hotel. Words delicate in courtesy and tentative in departure from formality passed between the two. And, as if in the expedient atmosphere of a real summer resort, an acquaintance grew, flowered and fructified on the spot as does the mystic plant of the conjuror. For a few moments they stood on a balcony upon which the corridor ended, and tossed the feathery ball of conversation.

'One tires of the old resorts,' said Madame Beaumont, with a faint but sweet smile. 'What is the use to fly to the mountains or the seashore to escape noise and dust when the very people that make both follow us there?'

'Even on the ocean,' remarked Farrington, sadly, 'the Philistines be upon you.* The most exclusive steamers are getting to be scarcely more than ferry boats. Heaven help us when the summer resorter discovers that the Lotus is further away from Broadway than Thousand Islands or Mackinac.'

'I hope our secret will be safe for a week, anyhow,' said Madame, with a sigh and a smile. 'I do not know where I would go if they should descend upon the dear Lotus. I know of but one place so delightful in summer, and that is the castle of Count Polinski, in the Ural Mountains.'

'I hear that Baden-Baden and Cannes are almost deserted this season,' said Farrington. 'Year by year the old resorts fall in disrepute. Perhaps many others, like ourselves, are seeking out the quiet nooks that are overlooked by the majority.'

'I promise myself three days more of this delicious rest,' said Madame Beaumont. 'On Monday the Cedric sails.'

Harold Farrington's eyes proclaimed his regret. 'I too must leave on Monday,' he said, 'but I do not go abroad.'

Madame Beaumont shrugged one round shoulder in a foreign gesture.

'One cannot bide here forever, charming though it may be. The chateau* has been in preparation for me longer than a month. Those house parties that one must give—what a nuisance! But I shall never forget my week in the Hotel Lotus.'

'Nor shall I,' said Farrington in a low voice, 'and I shall never forgive the Cedric.'

On Sunday evening, three days afterward, the two sat at a little table on the same balcony. A discreet waiter brought ices and small glasses of claret cup.

Madame Beaumont wore the same beautiful evening gown that she had worn each day at dinner. She seemed thoughtful. Near her hand on the table lay a small chatelaine* purse. After she had eaten her ice she opened the purse and took out a one-dollar bill.

'Mr Farrington,' she said, with the smile that had won the Hotel Lotus, 'I want to tell you something. I'm going to leave before breakfast in the morning because I've got to go back to my work. I'm behind the hosiery counter at Casey's Mammoth Store, and my vacation's up at eight o'clock tomorrow. That paper-dollar is the last cent I'll see till I draw my eight dollars salary next Saturday night. You're a real gentleman, and you've been good to me, and I wanted to tell you before I went. I've been saving up out of my wages for a year just for this vacation. I wanted to spend one week like a lady if I never do another one. I wanted to get up when I please instead of having to crawl out at seven every morning, and I wanted to live on the best and be waited on and ring bells for things just like rich folks do. Now I've done it, and I've had the happiest time I ever expect to have in my life. I'm going back to my work and my little hall bedroom satisfied for another year. I wanted to tell you about it, Mr Farrington, because I—I thought you kind of liked me, and I—I liked you. But, oh, I couldn't help deceiving you up till now, for it was all just like a fairy tale to me. So I talked about Europe and the things I've read about in other countries, and made you think I was a great lady.

'This dress I've got on—it's the only one I have that's fit to wear—I bought from O'Dowd & Levinsky on the installment plan.

'Seventy-five dollars is the price, and it was made to measure. I paid $10 down, and they're to collect $1 a week till it's paid for. That'll be about all I have to say, Mr Farrington, except that my name is Mamie Siviter instead of Madame Beaumont, and I thank you for your attentions. This dollar will pay the installment due on the dress to-morrow. I guess I'll go up to my room now.'

Harold Farrington listened to the recital of the Lotus's loveliest guest with an impassive countenance.* When she had concluded he drew a small book like a checkbook from his coat pocket. He wrote upon a blank form in this with a stub of pencil, tore out the leaf, tossed it over to his companion and took up the paper dollar.

'I've got to go to work, too, in the morning,' he said, 'and I might as well begin now. There's a receipt for the dollar instalment. I've been a collector for O'Dowd & Levinsky for three years. Funny, ain't it, that you and me both had the same idea about spending our vacation? I've always wanted to put up at a swell hotel, and I saved up out of my twenty per, and did it. Say, Mame, how about a trip to Coney Saturday night on the boat—what?'

The face of the pseudo Madame Heloise D'Arcy Beaumont beamed.

'Oh, you bet I'll go, Mr Farrington. The store closes at twelve on Saturdays. I guess Coney'll be all right even if we did spend a week with the swells.'

Below the balcony the sweltering city growled and buzzed in the July night. Inside the Hotel Lotus the tempered, cool shadows reigned, and the solicitous* waiter single-footed near the low windows, ready at a nod to serve Madame and her escort.

At the door of the elevator Farrington took his leave, and Madame Beaumont made her last ascent. But before they reached the noiseless cage be said: 'Just forget that "Harold Farrington," will you? McManus is the name—James McManus. Some call me Jimmy.'

'Good-night, Jimmy,' said Madame.

If you liked reading this story, you must also read:

The Gift of the Magi, After Twenty Years, The Last Leaf

GLOSSARY:

Adirondacks: A mountain range located in north-eastern Upstate New York, which is part of the United States

Caravansary: An inn, usually with a large courtyard, for the overnight accommodation of groups of travellers

Umbrageous: Shadowy

Pellucid: Translucently clear

Rapier: A very thin sword with a long sharp point

Rouge-et-noir: A gambling card game in which cards are turned up on a table marked with red and black diamonds

Purlieus: A term used for the outlying parts of a place or district
Inanition: Exhaustion caused by lack of nourishment
Nonpareil: Having no match or equal
Veracity: Accuracy
Patronym: A name derived from the name of a father or ancestor
Contiguous: Touching or sharing a common border
Freemasonry: An instinctive sympathy or fellow feeling between people with something in common
Acme: Peak or pinnacle
Conjuror: Illusionist or magician
Philistines be upon you: Biblical words of warning: be careful, watch out
Chateau: Castle or fortress
Claret: A type of red wine
Chatelaine: A set of short chains attached to a woman's belt, used for carrying keys or other items
Countenance: A person's face or facial expression
Solicitous: Eager or anxious to do something

Guy de Maupassant, France

(August 5, 1850 – July 6, 1893)

Guy de Maupassant wrote short stories and novels, and is considered one of the greatest French writers. His work is realistic and his characters occupy a world of material needs and sensual cravings. His characters are shown as victims of necessity who are crushed by their never ending fight against fate.

Henri René Albert Guy de Maupassant was born in a Norman, free-thinking family. After completing school, in the autumn of 1869, he started studying law. His law studies were, however, obstructed by the intervention of the Franco-Prussian War. Thus, the war serves as the backdrop for many of his stories.

He rose to prominence with Ball of Fat (1880). He published 300 short stories, six novels, and three travel books over the next ten years. His pieces, taken collectively, paint a comprehensive, vivid picture of French life from 1870 to 1890. He encapsulates war, the Norman peasantry, bureaucracy, life on the banks of the Seine, the emotional issues of the various classes.

The clarity of French with precise imagery forms the two aspects of Maupassant's appeal. Today, he is considered as one of the fathers of the modern short story as well as one of its finest practitioners. His legacy lies in the prolific and deeply admired body of work that influenced a great number of writers including William Somerset Maugham, O Henry, Anton Chekhov, Kate Chopin and Henry James.

Mother and Son

A party of men were chatting in the smoking room after dinner. We were talking of unexpected legacies, strange inheritances. Then M le Brument, who was sometimes called 'the illustrious judge' and at other times 'the illustrious lawyer,' went and stood with his back to the fire.

'I have,' said he, 'to search for an heir who disappeared under peculiarly distressing circumstances. It is one of those simple and terrible dramas of ordinary life, a thing which possibly happens every day, and which is nevertheless one of the most dreadful things I know. Here are the facts:

'Nearly six months ago I was called to the bedside of a dying woman. She said to me:

'"Monsieur, I want to intrust to you the most delicate, the most difficult, and the most wearisome mission that can be conceived. Be good enough to notice my will, which is there on the table. A sum of five thousand francs is left to you as a fee if you do not succeed, and of a hundred thousand francs if you do succeed. I want you to find my son after my death."

'She asked me to assist her to sit up in bed, in order that she might talk with greater ease, for her voice, broken and gasping, was whistling in her throat.

'It was a very wealthy establishment. The luxurious apartment, of an elegant simplicity, was upholstered* with materials as thick as walls, with a soft inviting surface.

'The dying woman continued:

'"You are the first to hear my horrible story. I will try to have strength enough to finish it. You must know all, in order that you, whom I know to be a kind-hearted man as well as a man of the world, may have a sincere desire to aid me with all your power.

'"Listen to me:

'"Before my marriage, I loved a young man, whose suit was rejected by my family because he was not rich enough. Not long afterward, I married a man of great wealth. I married him through ignorance, through obedience, through indifference, as young girls do marry.

'"I had a child, a boy. My husband died in the course of a few years.

'"He whom I had loved had married, in his turn. When he saw that I was a widow, he was crushed by grief at knowing he was not free. He came to see me; he wept and sobbed so bitterly, that it was enough to break my heart. He came to see me at first as a friend. Perhaps I ought not to have received him. What could I do? I was alone, so sad, so solitary, so hopeless! And I loved him still. What sufferings we women have sometimes to endure!

'"I had only him in the world, my parents being dead. He came frequently; he spent whole evenings with me. I should not have let him come so often, seeing that he was married. But I had not enough willpower to prevent him from coming.

'"How can I tell it?—he became my lover. How did this come about? Can I explain it? Can anyone explain such things? Do you think it could be otherwise when two human beings are drawn to each other by the irresistible force of mutual affection? Do you believe, monsieur, that it is always in our power to resist, that we can keep up the struggle forever, and refuse to yield to the prayers, the supplications,* the tears, the frenzied words, the appeals on bended knees, the transports of passion, with which we are pursued by the man we adore, whom we want to gratify even in his slightest wishes, whom we desire to crown with every possible happiness, and whom, if we are to be guided by a worldly code of honor, we must drive to despair? What strength would it not require? What a renunciation of happiness? What self-denial? And even what virtuous selfishness?

'"In short, monsieur, I was his mistress; and I was happy. I became—and this was my greatest weakness and my greatest piece of cowardice—I became his wife's friend.

'"We brought up my son together; we made a man of him, a thorough man, intelligent, full of sense and resolution, of large and generous ideas. The boy reached the age of seventeen.

'"He, the young man, was fond of my—my lover, almost as fond of him as I was myself, for he had been equally cherished and cared for by both of us. He used to call him his 'dear friend,' and respected him immensely, having never received from him anything but wise counsels and an example of integrity, honor, and probity.* He looked upon him as an old loyal and devoted comrade of his mother, as a sort of moral father, guardian, protector—how am I to describe it?

'"Perhaps the reason why he never asked any questions was that he had been accustomed from his earliest years to see this man in my house, at my side, and at his side, always concerned about us both.

'"One evening the three of us were to dine together—this was my chief amusement—and I waited for the two men, asking myself which of them would be the first to arrive. The door opened; it was my old friend. I went toward him, with outstretched arms; and he pressed my lips in a long, delicious kiss.

'"All of a sudden, a slight sound, a faint rustling, that mysterious sensation which indicates the presence of another person, made us start and turn round abruptly. Jean, my son, stood there, livid, staring at us.

'"There was a moment of atrocious confusion. I drew back, holding out my hand toward my son as if in supplication; but I could not see him. He had gone.

'"We remained facing each other—my lover and I—crushed, unable to utter a word. I sank into an armchair, and I felt a desire, a vague, powerful desire, to flee, to go out into the night, and to disappear forever. Then convulsive* sobs rose in my throat, and I wept, shaken with spasms, my heart breaking, all my nerves writhing with the horrible sensation of an irreparable, misfortune, and with that dreadful sense of shame which, in such moments as this, fills a mother's heart.

'"He looked at me in a terrified manner, not venturing to approach, to speak to me, or to touch me, for fear of the boy's return. At last, he said:

"''I am going to follow him to talk to him, to explain matters to him. In short, I must see him and let him know—'

"'And he hurried away.

"'I waited—waited in a distracted frame of mind, trembling at the least sound, starting with fear and with some unutterably strange and intolerable emotion at every slight crackling of the fire in the grate.

"'I waited an hour, two hours, feeling my heart swell with a dread I had never before experienced, such anguish that I would not wish the greatest criminal to endure ten minutes of such misery. Where was my son? What was he doing?

"'About midnight, a messenger brought me a note from my lover. I still know its contents by heart:

"'Has your son returned? I did not find him. I am down here. I do not want to go up at this hour.'

"'I wrote in pencil on the same slip of paper:

"'Jean has not returned. You must find him.'

"'And I 'remained all night in the armchair, waiting for him.

"'I felt as if I were going mad. I longed to run wildly about, to roll on the ground. And yet I did not even stir but kept waiting hour after hour. What was going to happen? I tried to imagine, to guess. But I could form no conception, in spite of my efforts, in spite of the tortures of my soul!

'"And now I feared that they might meet. What would they do in that case? What would my son do? My mind was torn with fearful doubts, with terrible suppositions.*

'"You can understand my feelings, can you not, monsieur?

'"My chambermaid, who knew nothing, who understood nothing, came into the room every moment, believing, naturally, that I had lost my reason. I sent her away with a word or a movement of the hand. She went for the doctor, who found me in the throes* of a nervous attack.

'"I was put to bed. I had brain fever.

'"When I regained consciousness, after a long illness, I saw beside my bed my—lover—alone.

'"I exclaimed:

'"My son? Where is my son?

'"He made no reply. I stammered:

'"Dead-dead. Has he committed suicide?

'"No, no, I swear it. But we have not found him in spite of all my efforts.

'"Then, becoming suddenly exasperated and even indignant—for women are subject to such outbursts of unaccountable and unreasoning anger—I said:

'"I forbid you to come near me or to see me again unless you find him. Go away!

'"He did go away.

'"I have never seen one or the other of them

since, monsieur, and thus I have lived for the last twenty years.

"'"Can you imagine what all this meant to me? Can you understand this monstrous punishment, this slow, perpetual laceration* of a mother's heart, this abominable, endless waiting? Endless, did I say? No; it is about to end, for I am dying. I am dying without ever again seeing either of them—either one or the other!

"'"He—the man I loved—has written to me every day for the last twenty years; and I—I have never consented to see him, even for one second; for I had a strange feeling that, if he were to come back here, my son would make his appearance at the same moment. Oh! My son! My son! Is he dead? Is he living? Where is he hiding? Over there, perhaps, beyond the great ocean, in some country so far away that even its very name is unknown to me! Does he ever think of me? Ah! If he only knew! How cruel one's children are! Did he understand to what frightful suffering he condemned me, into what depths of despair, into what tortures, he cast me while I was still in the prime of life, leaving me to suffer until this moment, when I am about to die—me, his mother, who loved him with all the intensity of a mother's love? Oh! Isn't it cruel, cruel?

"'"You will tell him all this, monsieur—will you not? You will repeat to him my last words:

'"My child, my dear, dear child, be less harsh toward poor women! Life is already brutal and savage enough in its dealings with them. My dear son, think of what the existence of your poor mother has been ever since the day you left her. My dear child, forgive her, and love her, now that she is dead, for she has had to endure the most frightful penance ever inflicted on a woman.'

'She gasped for breath, trembling, as if she had addressed the last words to her son and as if he stood by her bedside.

'Then she added:

'"You will tell him also, monsieur, that I never again saw the other."

'Once more she ceased speaking, then, in a broken voice, she said:

'"Leave me now, I beg of you. I want to die all alone since they are not with me."'

Maitre Le Brument added:

'And I left the house, monsieurs, crying like a fool, so bitterly, indeed, that my coachman turned round to stare at me.

'And to think that, every day, dramas like this are being enacted all around us!

'I have not found the son—that son—well, say what you like about him, but I call him that criminal son!'

If you liked reading this story, you must also read:

The Necklace, Mademoiselle Fifi, Miss Harriet

GLOSSARY:

Upholstered: Covered with cloth and filled with a soft substance

Supplications: A form of prayer, wherein one party humbly or earnestly asks another party to provide something

Probity: Integrity or honesty

Convulsive: Violent or jerky

Suppositions: An assumption or hypothesis

Throes: Intense or violent pain and struggle

Laceration: A deep cut or tear

Oscar Wilde, Ireland

(October 16, 1854 – November 30, 1900)

The Irish writer, Oscar Wilde, is known as an acclaimed poet and dramatist. He excelled as a journalist, author, short story writer, and essayist, proving that he could successfully write in just about any medium he chose.

Oscar Fingal O'Flahertie Wills Wilde was born to professional and literary genius people. He went on to attend Trinity College, Dublin, and later Oxford University, becoming widely known for his wit while still an undergraduate.

In the 1880s, he was a spokesman for the aesthetic movement called art for art's sake (*l'art pour l'art*).[1] He went on a lecture tour in the United States and became prominent in London circles for his sense and flamboyance. Despite his success, he became the focus of high-profile civil and criminal lawsuits involving homosexuality, which resulted in his imprisonment.

He explored gothic elements while mocking the bourgeois* morality in his only novel, *The Picture of Dorian Gray* (1891). He eventually established himself as the foremost dramatist of his era with his greatest work *The Importance of Being Earnest* (1899) that satirizes Victorian social hypocrisy.

He passed away young and destitute of acute meningitis. He was only forty-six years old. Today, his legacy goes beyond his written works as he is posthumously seen as a political symbol. Wilde was the most famous victim of the criminalization of homosexuality and as such, his plays took on a political tenor in the mid-twentieth century.

---

1 Art's for art's sake, also called *l'art pour l'art* in French, is a movement that pushes for the idea that art has an inherent value independent of its subject matter, or of any social, political, or ethical significance.

The Devoted Friend

One morning the old Water-rat put his head out of his hole. He had bright beady eyes and stiff grey whiskers and his tail was like a long bit of black india-rubber. The little ducks were swimming about in the pond, looking just like a lot of yellow canaries,* and their mother, who was pure white with real red legs, was trying to teach them how to stand on their heads in the water.

'You will never be in the best society unless you can stand on your heads,' she kept saying to them; and every now and then she showed them how it was done. But the little ducks paid no attention to her. They were so young that they did not know what an advantage it is to be in society at all.

'What disobedient children!' cried the old

Water-rat; 'they really deserve to be drowned.'

'Nothing of the kind,' answered the Duck, 'every one must make a beginning, and parents cannot be too patient.'

'Ah! I know nothing about the feelings of parents,' said the Water-rat; 'I am not a family man. In fact, I have never been married, and I never intend to be. Love is all very well in its way, but friendship is much higher. Indeed, I know of nothing in the world that is either nobler or rarer than a devoted friendship.'

'And what, pray, is your idea of the duties of a devoted friend?' asked a Green Linnet, who was sitting in a willow-tree hard by, and had overheard the conversation.

'Yes, that is just what I want to know,' said the Duck; and she swam away to the end of the pond, and stood upon her head, in order to give her children a good example.

'What a silly question!' cried the Water-rat. 'I should expect my devoted friend to be devoted to me, of course.'

'And what would you do in return?' said the little bird, swinging upon a silver spray, and flapping his tiny wings.

'I don't understand you,' answered the Water-rat.

'Let me tell you a story on the subject,' said the Linnet.

'Is the story about me?' asked the Water-rat. If so, I will listen to it, for I am extremely fond of fiction.'

'It is applicable to you,' answered the Linnet; and he flew down, and alighting upon the bank, he told the story of The Devoted Friend.

• • •

'Once upon a time,' said the Linnet, 'there was an honest little fellow named Hans.'

'Was he very distinguished?' asked the Water-rat.

'No,' answered the Linnet, I don't think he was distinguished at all, except for his kind heart, and his funny round good-humoured face. He lived in a tiny cottage all by himself, and every day he worked in his garden. In all the country-side there was no garden so lovely as his. Sweet-william grew there, and Gilly-flowers, and Shepherds'-purses, and Fair-maids of France. There were damask Roses, and yellow Roses, lilac Crocuses, and gold, purple Violets and white. Columbine and Ladysmock, Marjoram and Wild Basil, the Cowslip and the Flower-de-luce, the Daffodil and the Clove-Pink bloomed or blossomed in their proper order as the months went by, one flower taking another flower's place, so that there were always beautiful things to look at, and pleasant odours to smell.

Little Hans had a great many friends, but

the most devoted friend of all was big Hugh the Miller. Indeed, so devoted was the rich Miller to little Hans, that he would never go by his garden without leaning over the wall and plucking a large nosegay,* or a handful of sweet herbs, or filling his pockets with plums and cherries if it was the fruit season.

'Real friends should have everything in common,' the Miller used to say, and little Hans nodded and smiled, and felt very proud of having a friend with such noble ideas.

Sometimes, indeed, the neighbours thought it strange that the rich Miller never gave little Hans anything in return, though he had a hundred sacks of flour stored away in his mill, and six milch cows, and a large flock of woolly sheep; but Hans never troubled his head about these things, and nothing gave him greater pleasure than to listen to all the wonderful things the Miller used to say about the unselfishness of true friendship.

So little Hans worked away in his garden. During the spring, the summer, and the autumn he was very happy, but when the winter came, and he had no fruit or flowers to bring to the market, he suffered a good deal from cold and hunger, and often had to go to bed without any supper but a few dried pears or some hard nuts. In the winter, also, he was extremely lonely, as the Miller never came to see him then.

'There is no good in my going to see little Hans as long as the snow lasts,' the Miller used to say to his wife, 'for when people are in trouble they should be left alone, and not be bothered by visitors. That at least is my idea about friendship, and I am sure I am right. So I shall wait till the spring comes, and then I shall pay him a visit, and he will be able to give me a large basket of primroses, and that will make him so happy.'

'You are certainly very thoughtful about others,' answered the Wife, as she sat in her comfortable armchair by the big pinewood fire; 'very thoughtful indeed. It is quite a treat to hear you talk about friendship. I am sure the clergyman* himself could not say such beautiful things as you do, though he does live in a three-storied house, and wear a gold ring on his little finger.'

'But could we not ask little Hans up here?' said the Miller's youngest son. 'If poor Hans is in trouble I will give him half my porridge* and show him my white rabbits.'

'What a silly boy you are!' cried the Miller; 'I really don't know what is the use of sending you to school. You seem not to learn anything. Why, if little Hans came up here, and saw our warm fire, and our good supper, and our great cask of red wine, he might get envious, and envy is a most terrible thing, and would spoil anybody's nature. I certainly will not allow Hans's nature to be spoiled.

I am his best friend, and I will always watch over him, and see that he is not led into any temptations. Besides, if Hans came here, he might ask me to let him have some flour on credit, and that I could not do. Flour is one thing, and friendship is another, and they should not be confused. Why, the words are spelt differently and mean quite different things. Everybody can see that.'

'How well you talk!' said the Miller's Wife, pouring herself out a large glass of warm ale; 'really I feel quite drowsy. It is just like being in church.'

'Lots of people act well,' answered the Miller; 'but very few people talk well, which shows that talking is much the more difficult thing of the two, and much the finer thing also'; and he looked sternly across the table at his little son, who felt so ashamed of himself that he hung his head down, and grew quite scarlet, and began to cry into his tea. However, he was so young that you must excuse him.

• • •

'Is that the end of the story?' asked the Water-rat.

'Certainly not,' answered the Linnet; 'that is the beginning.'

'Then you are quite behind the age,' said the Water-rat. 'Every good storyteller nowadays starts with the end, and then goes on to the beginning, and concludes with the middle. That is the new method. I heard all about it the other day from a critic who was walking round the pond with a young man. He spoke of the matter at great length, and I am sure he must have been right, for he had blue spectacles and a bald head, and whenever the young man made any remark, he always answered 'Pooh!' But pray go on with your story. I like the Miller immensely. I have all kinds of beautiful sentiments myself, so there is a great sympathy between us.'

• • •

'Well,' said the Linnet, hopping now on one leg and now on the other, 'as soon as the winter was over, and the primroses began to open their pale yellow stars, the Miller said to his wife that he would go down and see little Hans.

'Why, what a good heart you have!' cried his Wife; 'you are always thinking of others. And mind you take the big basket with you for the flowers.'

'So the Miller tied the sails of the windmill together with a strong iron chain, and went down the hill with the basket on his arm.

'Good morning, little Hans,' said the Miller.

'Good morning,' said Hans, leaning on his spade, and smiling from ear to ear.

'And how have you been all the winter?' said the Miller. 'Well, really,' cried Hans, 'it is very good of you to ask, very good indeed. I am afraid I had rather a hard time of it, but now the spring has come, and I am quite happy, and all my flowers are doing well.'

'We often talked of you during the winter, Hans,' said the Miller, 'and wondered how you were getting on.'

'That was kind of you,' said Hans; 'I was half afraid you had forgotten me.'

'Hans, I am surprised at you,' said the Miller; 'friendship never forgets. That is the wonderful thing about it, but I am afraid you don't understand the poetry of life. How lovely your primroses are looking, by-the-bye!'

'They are certainly very lovely,' said Hans, 'and it is a most lucky thing for me that I have so many. I am going to bring them into the market and sell them to the Burgomaster's daughter, and buy back my wheelbarrow with the money.'

'Buy back your wheelbarrow? You don't mean to say you have sold it? What a very stupid thing to do!'

'Well, the fact is,' said Hans, 'that I was obliged to. You see the winter was a very bad time for me, and I really had no money at all to buy bread with. So I first sold the silver buttons off my Sunday coat, and then I sold my silver chain, and then I sold my big pipe, and at last I sold my wheelbarrow. But I am going to buy them all back again now.'

'Hans,' said the Miller, 'I will give you my wheelbarrow. It is not in very good repair; indeed, one side is gone, and there is something wrong with the wheel-spokes; but in spite of that I will give it to you. I know it is very generous of me, and a great many people would think me extremely foolish for parting with it, but I am not like the rest of the world. I think that generosity is the essence of friendship, and, besides, I have got a new wheelbarrow for myself. Yes, you may set your mind at ease, I will give you my wheelbarrow.'

'Well, really, that is generous of you,' said little Hans, and his funny round face glowed all over with pleasure. 'I can easily put it in repair, as I have a plank of wood in the house.'

'A plank of wood' said the Miller; 'why, that is just what I want for the roof of my barn. There is a very large hole in it, and the corn will all get damp if I don't stop it up. How lucky you mentioned it! It is quite remarkable how one good action always breeds another. I have given you my wheelbarrow, and now you are going to give me your plank. Of course, the wheelbarrow is worth far more than the plank, but true friendship never notices things like that. Pray get it at once, and I will set to work at my barn this very day.'

'Certainly,' cried little Hans, and he ran into the shed and dragged the plank out.

'It is not a very big plank,' said the Miller,

looking at it, 'and I am afraid that after I have mended my barn-roof there won't be any left for you to mend the wheelbarrow with; but, of course, that is not my fault. And now, as I have given you my wheelbarrow, I am sure you would like to give me some flowers in return. Here is the basket, and mind you fill it quite full.'

'Quite full?' said little Hans, rather sorrowfully, for it was really a very big basket, and he knew that if he filled it he would have no flowers left for the market and he was very anxious to get his silver buttons back.

'Well, really,' answered the Miller, 'as I have given you my wheelbarrow, I don't think that it is much to ask you for a few flowers. I may be wrong, but I should have thought that friendship, true friendship, was quite free from selfishness of any kind.'

'My dear friend, my best friend,' cried little Hans, 'you are welcome to all the flowers in my garden. I would much sooner have your good opinion than my silver buttons, any day;' and he ran and plucked all his pretty primroses, and filled the Miller's basket.

'Good-bye, little Hans,' said the Miller, as he went up the hill with the plank on his shoulder, and the big basket in his hand.

'Good-bye,' said little Hans, and he began to dig away quite merrily, he was so pleased about the wheelbarrow.

The next day he was nailing up some honeysuckle* against the porch, when he heard the Miller's voice calling to him from the road. So he jumped off the ladder, and ran down the garden, and looked over the wall.

There was the Miller with a large sack of flour on his back.

'Dear little Hans,' said the Miller, 'would you mind carrying this sack of flour for me to market?'

'Oh, I am so sorry,' said Hans, 'but I am really very busy to-day. I have got all my creepers to nail up, and all my flowers to water, and all my grass to roll.'

'Well, really,' said the Miller, 'I think that, considering that I am going to give you my wheelbarrow, it is rather unfriendly of you to refuse.'

'Oh, don't say that,' cried little Hans, 'I wouldn't be unfriendly for the whole world'; and he ran in for his cap, and trudged off with the big sack on his shoulders.

It was a very hot day, and the road was terribly dusty, and before Hans had reached the sixth milestone he was so tired that he had to sit down and rest. However, he went on bravely, and at last he reached the market. After he had waited there some time, he sold the sack of flour for a very good price, and then he returned home at once, for he was afraid that if he stopped too late he might meet some robbers on the way.

'It has certainly been a hard day,' said little Hans to himself as he was going to bed, 'but I am glad I did not refuse the Miller, for he is my best friend, and, besides, he is going to give me his wheelbarrow.'

Early the next morning the Miller came down to get the money for his sack of flour, but little Hans was so tired that he was still in bed.

'Upon my word,' said the Miller, 'you are very lazy. Really, considering that I am going to give you my wheelbarrow, I think you might work harder. Idleness is a great sin, and I certainly don't like any of my friends to be idle or sluggish. You must not mind my speaking quite plainly to you. Of course I should not dream of doing so if I were not your friend. But what is the good of friendship if one cannot say exactly what one means? Anybody can say charming things and try to please and to flatter, but a true friend always says unpleasant things, and does not mind giving pain. Indeed, if he is a really true friend he prefers it, for he knows that then he is doing good.'

'I am very sorry,' said little Hans, rubbing his eyes and pulling off his night-cap, 'but I was so tired that I thought I would lie in bed for a little time, and listen to the birds singing. Do you know that I always work better after hearing the birds sing?'

'Well, I am glad of that,' said the Miller, clapping little Hans on the back, 'for I want you to come up to the mill as soon as you are dressed, and mend my barn-roof for me.'

Poor little Hans was very anxious to go and work in his garden, for his flowers had not been watered for two days, but he did not like to refuse the Miller, as he was such a good friend to him.

'Do you think it would be unfriendly of me if I said I was busy?' he inquired in a shy and timid voice.

'Well, really,' answered the Miller, 'I do not think it is much to ask of you, considering that I am going to give you my wheelbarrow; but of course if you refuse I will go and do it myself.'

'Oh! on no account,' cried little Hans and he jumped out of bed, and dressed himself, and went up to the barn.

He worked there all day long, till sunset, and at sunset the Miller came to see how he was getting on.

'Have you mended the hole in the roof yet, little Hans?' cried the Miller in a cheery voice.

'It is quite mended,' answered little Hans, coming down the ladder.

'Ah!' said the Miller, 'there is no work so delightful as the work one does for others.'

'It is certainly a great privilege to hear you talk,'answered little Hans, sitting down and wiping his forehead, 'a very great privilege. But I am afraid

I shall never have such beautiful ideas as you have.'

'Oh! they will come to you,' said the Miller, 'but you must take more pains. At present you have only the practice of friendship; some day you will have the theory also.'

'Do you really think I shall?' asked little Hans.

'I have no doubt of it,' answered the Miller; 'but now that you have mended the roof, you had better go home and rest, for I want you to drive my sheep to the mountain to-morrow.'

Poor little Hans was afraid to say anything to this, and early the next morning the Miller brought his sheep round to the cottage, and Hans started off with them to the mountain. It took him the whole day to get there and back; and when he returned he was so tired that he went off to sleep in his chair, and did not wake up till it was broad daylight.

'What a delightful time I shall have in my garden,' he said, and he went to work at once.

But somehow he was never able to look after his flowers at all, for his friend the Miller was always coming round and sending him off on long errands, or getting him to help at the mill. Little Hans was very much distressed at times, as he was afraid his flowers would think he had forgotten them, but he consoled himself by the reflection that the Miller was his best friend. 'Besides,' he used to say, 'he is going to give me his wheelbarrow, and that is an act of pure generosity.'

So little Hans worked away for the Miller, and the Miller said all kinds of beautiful things about friendship, which Hans took down in a note-book, and used to read over at night, for he was a very good scholar.

Now it happened that one evening little Hans was sitting by his fireside when a loud rap came at the door. It was a very wild night, and the wind was blowing and roaring round the house so terribly that at first he thought it was merely the storm. But a second rap came, and then a third, louder than any of the others.

'It is some poor traveller,' said little Hans to himself, and he ran to the door.

There stood the Miller with a lantern in one hand and a big stick in the other.

'Dear little Hans,' cried the Miller, 'I am in great trouble. My little boy has fallen off a ladder and hurt himself, and I am going for the Doctor. But he lives so far away, and it is such a bad night, that it has just occurred to me that it would be much better if you went instead of me. You know I am going to give you my wheelbarrow, and so, it is only fair that you should do something for me in return.'

'Certainly,' cried little Hans, 'I take it quite as a compliment your coming to me, and I will start off at once. But you must lend me your lantern, as the night is so dark that I am afraid I might fall into the ditch.'

'I am very sorry,' answered the Miller, 'but it is my new lantern, and it would be a great loss to me if anything happened to it.'

'Well, never mind, I will do without it,' cried little Hans, and he took down his great fur coat, and his warm scarlet cap, and tied a muffler round his throat, and started off.

What a dreadful storm it was! The night was so black that little Hans could hardly see, and the wind was so strong that he could scarcely stand. However, he was very courageous, and after he had been walking about three hours, he arrived at the Doctor's house, and knocked at the door.

'Who is there?' cried the Doctor, putting his head out of his bedroom window.

'Little Hans, Doctor.'

'What do you want, little Hans?'

'The Miller's son has fallen from a ladder, and has hurt himself, and the Miller wants you to come at once.'

'All right!' said the Doctor; and he ordered his horse, and his big boots, and his lantern, and came downstairs, and rode off in the direction of the Miller's house, little Hans trudging behind him.

But the storm grew worse and worse, and the rain fell in torrents, and little Hans could not see where he was going, or keep up with the horse. At last he lost his way, and wandered off on the moor,* which was a very dangerous place, as it was full of deep holes, and there poor little Hans was drowned. His body was found the next day by some goatherds, floating in a great pool of water, and was brought back by them to the cottage.

Everybody went to little Hans's funeral, as he was so popular, and the Miller was the chief mourner.

'As I was his best friend,' said the Miller, 'it is only fair that I should have the best place;' so he walked at the head of the procession in a long black cloak, and every now and then he wiped his eyes with a big pocket-handkerchief.

'Little Hans is certainly a great loss to every one,' said the Blacksmith, when the funeral was over, and they were all seated comfortably in the inn, drinking spiced wine and eating sweet cakes.

'A great loss to me at any rate,' answered the Miller, 'why I had as good as given him my wheelbarrow, and now I really don't know what to do with it. It is very much in my way at home, and it is in such bad repair that I could not get anything for it if I sold it. I will certainly take care not to give away anything again. One always suffers for being generous.'

• • •

'Well?' said the Water-rat, after a long pause.

'Well, that is the end,' said the Linnet.

'But what became of the Miller?' asked the Water-rat. 'Oh! I really don't know,' replied the

Linnet, 'and I am sure that I don't care.'

'It is quite evident then that you have no sympathy in your nature,' said the Water-rat.

'I am afraid you don't quite see the moral of the story,' remarked the Linnet.

'The what?' screamed the Water-rat.

'The moral.'

'Do you mean to say that the story has a moral?'

'Certainly,' said the Linnet.

'Well, really,' said the Water-rat, in a very angry manner, 'I think you should have told me that before you began. If you had done so, I certainly would not have listened to you; in fact, I should have said "Pooh," like the critic. However, I can say it now;' so he shouted out 'Pooh' at the top of his voice, gave a whisk with his tail, and went back into his hole.

'And how do you like the Water-rat?' asked the Duck, who came paddling up some minutes afterwards. 'He has a great many good points, but for my own part I have a mother's feelings, and I can never look at a confirmed bachelor without the tears coming into my eyes.'

'I am rather afraid that I have annoyed him,' answered the Linnet. 'The fact is, that I told him a story with a moral.'

'Ah! That is always a very dangerous thing to do,' said the Duck.

And I quite agree with her.

If you liked reading this story, you must also read:

The Happy Prince, Lord Arthur Savile's Crime, The Portrait of Mr W H

GLOSSARY:

Bourgeois: Belonging to middle-class
Canaries: A type of bird that is bright yellow in colour
Nosegay: Small bunch of flowers, typically one that is sweet-scented
Clergyman: Male priest or religious leader of Christians
Porridge: Dish consisting of oatmeal or another meal or cereal boiled in water or milk
Honeysuckle: A climbing plant with flowers that smell sweet
Moor: An expanse of open rolling infertile land

Anton Chekhov, Russia

(January 29, 1860 – July 15, 1904)

Anton Chekhov, the great Russian writer, is considered to be the master of the modern short story. He was a literary artist of austere* accuracy who explored the depths of the surface of life, revealing his characters' inner motivations. Chekhov's best plays and short tales are devoid of sophisticated storylines and elegant conclusions. By focusing on seemingly little details, he produces one-of-a-kind atmosphere that has been described as frightening or lyrical.

Anton Pavlovich Chekhov was born in Taganrog, a tiny seaport. As a young adult, he studied medicine and also took on financial responsibility for the family which led him to author and sell a huge number of hilarious stories and vignettes on current Russian life. By the age of twenty-six, he had published over 400 short tales, drawings, and vignettes. His experiments with serious writing provide the studies of human misery and despair strangely at variance with the frenzied facetiousness* of his comic work. Gradually, that former attained dominance over the comic.

In 1904, Chekhov died due to the complications of tuberculosis. His well-known works of short fiction are *Ward No. 6* (1892), *The Darling* (1899), *Gusev* (1890), and *The Lady with the Little Dog* (1899). His legacy follows the length of writers that he has inspired over the years and who went on to make a name for themselves, like Ernest Hemingway, Tennessee Williams and Henry Miller.

In An Hotel

'Let me tell you, my good man,' began Madame Nashatyrin, the colonel's lady at No. 47, crimson and spluttering, as she pounced on the hotel-keeper. 'Either give me other apartments, or I shall leave your confounded* hotel altogether! It's a sink of iniquity!* Mercy on us, I have grown-up daughters and one hears nothing but abominations* day and night! It's beyond everything! Day and night! Sometimes he fires off such things that it simply makes one's ears blush! Positively like a cabman. It's a good thing that my poor girls don't understand or I should have to fly out into the street with them. ... He's saying something now! You listen!'

'I know a thing better than that, my boy,' a husky bass floated in from the next room. 'Do you remember Lieutenant Druzhkov? Well, that same Druzhkov was one day making a drive with the yellow into the pocket and as he usually did, you know, flung up his leg. … All at once something went crrr-ack! At first they thought he had torn the cloth of the billiard table, but when they looked, my dear fellow, his United States had split at every seam! He had made such a high kick, the beast, that not a seam was left. … Ha-ha-ha, and there were ladies present, too … among others the wife of that drivelling* Lieutenant Okurin. … Okurin was furious. … 'How dare the fellow,' said he, 'behave with impropriety in the presence of my wife?' One thing led to another … you know our fellows! … Okurin sent seconds to Druzhkov, and Druzhkov said 'don't be a fool' … ha-ha-ha, 'but tell him he had better send seconds not to me but to the tailor who made me those breeches; it is his fault, you know.' Ha-ha-ha! Ha-ha-ha. …'

Lilya and Mila, the colonel's daughters, who were sitting in the window with their round cheeks propped on their fists, flushed crimson and dropped their eyes that looked buried in their plump faces.

'Now you have heard him, haven't you?' Madame Nashatyrin went on, addressing the hotel-keeper. 'And that, you consider, of no consequence, I suppose? I am the wife of a colonel, sir! My husband is a commanding officer. I will not permit some cabman to utter such infamies almost in my presence!'

'He is not a cabman, madam, but the staff-captain Kikin. … A gentleman born.'

'If he has so far forgotten his station as to express himself like a cabman, then he is even more deserving of contempt!* In short, don't answer me, but kindly take steps!'

'But what can I do, madam? You are not the only one to complain, everybody's complaining, but what am I to do with him? One goes to his room and begins putting him to shame, saying: 'Hannibal Ivanitch, have some fear of God! It's shameful! and he'll punch you in the face with his fists and say all sorts of things: 'there, put that in your pipe and smoke it,' and such like. It's a disgrace! He wakes up in the morning and sets to walking about the corridor in nothing, saving your presence, but his underclothes. And when he has had a drop he will pick up a revolver and set to putting bullets into the wall. By day he is swilling* liquor and at night he plays cards like mad, and after cards it is fighting. … I am ashamed for the other lodgers to see it!'

'Why don't you get rid of the scoundrel?'

'Why, there's no getting him out! He owes me for three months, but we don't ask for our money, we simply ask him to get out as a favour.

... The magistrate has given him an order to clear out of the rooms, but he's taking it from one court to another, and so it drags on. ... He's a perfect nuisance, that's what he is. And, good Lord, such a man, too! Young, good-looking and intellectual. ... When he hasn't had a drop you couldn't wish to see a nicer gentleman. The other day he wasn't drunk and he spent the whole day writing letters to his father and mother.'

'Poor father and mother!' sighed the colonel's lady.

'They are to be pitied, to be sure! There's no comfort in having such a scamp!* He's sworn at and turned out of his lodgings, and not a day passes but he is in trouble over some scandal. It's sad!'

'His poor unhappy wife!' sighed the lady.

'He has no wife, madam. A likely idea! She would have to thank God if her head were not broken. ...'

The lady walked up and down the room.

'He is not married, you say?'

'Certainly not, madam.'

The lady walked up and down the room again and mused a little.

'H'm, not married. ...' she pronounced meditatively. 'H'm. Lilya and Mila, don't sit at the window, there's a draught! What a pity! A young man and to let himself sink to this! And all owing to what? The lack of good influence! There is no mother who would. ... Not married? Well ... there it is. ... Please be so good,' the lady continued suavely after a moment's thought, 'as to go to him and ask him in my name to ... refrain from using expressions. ... Tell him that Madame Nashatyrin begs him. … Tell him she is staying with her daughters in No. 47 … that she has come up from her estate in the country. ...'

'Certainly.'

'Tell him, a colonel's lady and her daughters. He might even come and apologize. ... We are always at home after dinner. Oh, Mila, shut the window!'

'Why, what do you want with that ... black sheep, mamma?' drawled Lilya when the hotel-keeper had retired. 'A queer person to invite! A drunken, rowdy rascal!'

'Oh, don't say so, *ma chère*! You always talk like that; and there … sit down! Why, whatever he may be, we ought not to despise him. ... There's something good in everyone. Who knows,' sighed the colonel's lady, looking her daughters up and down anxiously, 'perhaps your fate is here. Change your dresses anyway. …'

If you liked reading this story, you must also read:

The Grasshopper, Ward No. 6, The Two Volodyas

Glossary:

Austere: Plain or unadorned appearance
Facetiousness: Joking or jesting often inappropriately
Confounded: Used for emphasis, especially to express anger or annoyance
Iniquity: Immoral or grossly unfair behaviour
Abominations: An action that causes disgust or loathing
Drivelling: Babbling or talking nonsense
Contempt: Worthless or beneath consideration
Swilling: To drink greedily or in large quantities
Scamp: A wicked or worthless person

Frances Harper, USA

(September 24, 1825 – February 22, 1911)

The African American writer, Frances Harper, was not only the first African-American woman to publish a short story, but she was also an influential abolitionist,* suffragist,* and reformer that co-founded the National Association of Colored Women's Clubs.

Frances Ellen Watkins Harper was born in Baltimore, Maryland to free African American parents. An only child, she lost her parents at the age of three. She was raised by her aunt and uncle who sent her to attend the Watkins Academy until she was thirteen years old. At that age, children were typically expected to join the workforce so she took a job as a nursemaid and seamstress for a white family that owned a bookshop. This is where her love for books was cultivated. By the age of twenty-one, Harper wrote her first small volume of poetry, called *Forest Leaves* (1845).

Harper could no longer return to her own house at twenty-six years of age.[1] This is when she decided to devote her entire life to

1 Harper could not return to Maryland because the American society was still divided over race in a system called segregation that kept people apart. This discrimination led to unjust laws that denied the entry of free African Americans from the north to enter the state.

the antislavery fight. Her poem *Eliza Harris* was published in The Liberator and Frederick Douglass' Paper. By 1854, she had compiled her second small volume of poetry called *Poems on Miscellaneous Subjects* that had an introduction by abolitionist William Lloyd Garrison.

For the next eight years, Harper travelled across the United States and Canada as a lecturer. Beyond this, Harper was committed to the struggle for women's rights and the temperance movement. Her short story, *The Two Offers* was published in 1859, in an Anglo-African Magazine and became the first short story published by an African American woman.

She passed away in 1911 and left behind a canon of ingenious works to inspire people around the world. Her influence led to the foundation of the American Equal Rights Association that would advocate for both women's and African American suffrage.

The Two Offers

'What is the matter with you, Laura, this morning? I have been watching you this hour, and in that time you have commenced a half dozen letters and torn them all up. What matter of such grave moment is puzzling your dear little head, that you do not know how to decide?'

'Well, it is an important matter: I have two offers for marriage, and I do not know which to choose.'

'I should accept neither, or to say the least, not at present.'

'Why not?'

'Because I think a woman who is undecided between two offers, has not love enough for either to make a choice; and in that very hesitation, indecision, she has a reason to pause and seriously reflect, lest her marriage, instead of being an affinity* of souls or a union of hearts, should only be a mere matter of bargain and sale, or an affair of convenience and selfish interest.'

'But I consider them both very good offers, just such as many a girl would gladly receive. But to tell you the truth, I do not think that I regard either as a woman should the man she chooses for her husband. But then if I refuse, there is the risk of being an old maid, and that is not to be thought of.'

'Well, suppose there is, is that the most dreadful fate that can befall a woman? Is there not more intense wretchedness in an ill-assorted marriage—more utter loneliness in a loveless home, than in the lot of the old maid who accepts her earthly mission as a gift from God, and strives to walk the path of life with earnest and unfaltering steps?'

'Oh! what a little preacher you are. I really believe that you were cut out for an old maid; that when nature formed you, she put in a double portion of intellect to make up for a deficiency of love; and yet you are kind and affectionate. But I do not think that you know anything of the grand, over-mastering passion, or the deep necessity of woman's heart for loving.'

'Do you think so?' resumed the first speaker; and bending over her work she quietly applied herself to the knitting that had lain neglected by her side, during this brief conversation; but as she did so, a shadow flitted over her pale and intellectual brow, a mist gathered in her eyes, and a slight quivering of the lips, revealed a depth of feeling to which her companion was a stranger.

But before I proceed with my story, let me give you a slight history of the speakers. They were cousins, who had met life under different auspices.* Laura Lagrange, was the only daughter of rich and indulgent parents, who had spared no pains to make her an accomplished lady.

Her cousin, Janette Alston, was the child of parents, rich only in goodness and affection. Her father had been unfortunate in business, and dying before he could retrieve his fortunes, left his business in an embarrassed state.

His widow was unacquainted with his business affairs, and when the estate was settled, hungry creditors had brought their claims and the lawyers had received their fees, she found herself homeless and almost penniless, and she who had been sheltered in the warm clasp of loving arms, found them too powerless to shield her from the pitiless pelting storms of adversity.

Year after year she struggled with poverty and wrestled with want, till her toil-worn hands became too feeble to hold the shattered chords of existence, and her tear-dimmed eyes grew heavy with the slumber of death.

Her daughter had watched over her with untiring devotion, had closed her eyes in death, and gone out into the busy, restless world, missing a precious tone from the voices of earth, a beloved step from the paths of life.

Too self reliant to depend on the charity of relations, she endeavored to support herself by her own exertions, and she had succeeded. Her path for a while was marked with struggle and trial, but instead of uselessly repining, she met them bravely, and her life became not a thing of ease and indulgence, but of conquest, victory, and accomplishments.

At the time when this conversation took place, the deep trials of her life had passed away. The achievements of her genius had won her a position in the literary world, where she shone as one of its bright particular stars. And with her fame came a competence of worldly means, which gave her leisure for improvement, and the riper development of her rare talents.

And she, that pale intellectual woman, whose genius gave life and vivacity to the social circle, and whose presence threw a halo of beauty and grace around the charmed atmosphere in which she moved, had at one period of her life, known the mystic and solemn strength of an all-absorbing love. Years faded into the misty past, had seen the kindling of her eye, the quick flushing of her cheek, and the wild throbbing of her heart, at tones of a voice long since hushed to the stillness of death.

Deeply, wildly, passionately, she had loved. Her whole life seemed like the pouring out of rich, warm and gushing affections. This love quickened her talents, inspired her genius, and threw over her life a tender and spiritual earnestness. And then came a fearful shock, a mournful waking from that "dream of beauty and delight."

A shadow fell around her path; it came between her and the object of her heart's worship; first a few cold words, estrangement, and then a painful separation; the old story of woman's pride—digging the sepulchre* of her happiness, and then a new-made grave, and her path over it to the spirit world; and thus faded out from that young heart her bright, brief and saddened dream of life.

Faint and spirit-broken, she turned from the scenes associated with the memory of the loved and lost. She tried to break the chain of sad associations that bound her to the mournful past; and so, pressing back the bitter sobs from her almost breaking heart, like the dying dolphin, whose beauty is born of its death anguish, her genius gathered strength from suffering and wondrous power and brilliancy from the agony she hid within the desolate chambers of her soul.

Men hailed her as one of earth's strangely gifted children, and wreathed the garlands of fame for her brow, when it was throbbing with a wild and fearful unrest. They breathed her name with applause, when through the lonely halls of her stricken spirit, was an earnest cry for peace, a deep yearning for sympathy and heart-support.

But life, with its stern realities, met her; its solemn responsibilities confronted her, and turning, with an earnest and shattered spirit, to life's duties and trials, she found a calmness and strength that she had only imagined in her dreams of poetry and song.

We will now pass over a period of ten years, and the cousins have met again. In that calm and lovely woman, in whose eyes is a depth of tenderness, tempering the flashes of her genius, whose looks and tones are full of sympathy and love, we recognize the once smitten and stricken Janette Alston.

The bloom of her girlhood had given way to a higher type of spiritual beauty, as if some unseen hand had been polishing and refining the temple in which her lovely spirit found its habitation; and this had been the fact. Her inner life had grown beautiful, and it was this that was constantly developing the outer.

Never, in the early flush of womanhood, when an absorbing love had lit up her eyes and glowed in her life, had she appeared so interesting as when, with a countenance which seemed overshadowed with a spiritual light, she bent over the death-bed of a young woman, just lingering at the shadowy gates of the unseen land.

'Has he come?' faintly but eagerly exclaimed the dying woman. 'Oh! how I have longed for his coming, and even in death he forgets me.'

'Oh, do not say so, dear Laura, some accident may have detained him,' said Janette to her cousin; for on that bed, from whence she will never rise, lies the once-beautiful and lighthearted Laura Lagrange, the brightness of whose eyes has long since been dimmed with tears, and whose voice had become like a harp whose every chord is turned to sadness—whose faintest thrill and loudest vibrations are but the variations of agony.

A heavy hand was laid upon her once warm and bounding heart, and a voice came whispering through her soul, that she must die. But, to her, the tidings was a message of deliverance—a voice, hushing her wild sorrows to the calmness of resignation and hope. Life had grown so weary upon her head— the future looked so hopeless— she had no wish to tread again the track where thorns had pierced her feet, and clouds overcast her sky; and she hailed the coming of death's angel as the footsteps of a welcome friend.

And yet, earth had one object so very dear to her weary heart. It was her absent and 4 recreant husband; for, since that conversation, she had accepted one of her offers, and become a wife. But, before she married, she learned that great lesson of human experience and woman's life, to love the man who bowed at her shrine, a willing worshipper.

He had a pleasing address, raven hair, flashing eyes, a voice of thrilling sweetness, and lips of persuasive eloquence;* and being well versed in the ways of the world, he won his way to her heart, and she became his bride, and he was proud of his prize.

Vain and superficial in his character, he looked upon marriage not as a divine sacrament for the soul's development and human progression, but as the title-deed that gave him possession of the woman he thought he loved.

But alas for her, the laxity of his principles had rendered him unworthy of the deep and undying devotion of a pure-hearted woman; but, for awhile, he hid from her his true character, and she blindly loved him, and for a short period was happy in the consciousness of being beloved; though sometimes a vague unrest would fill her soul, when, overflowing with a sense of the good, the beautiful, and the true, she would turn to him, but find no response to the deep yearnings of her soul—no appreciation of life's highest realities—its solemn grandeur and significant importance.

Their souls never met, and soon she found a void in her bosom, that his earth-born love could not fill. He did not satisfy the wants of her mental and moral nature—between him and her there was no affinity of minds, no intercommunion of souls.

Talk as you will of woman's deep capacity for loving, of the strength of her affectional nature. I do not deny it; but will the mere possession of any human love, fully satisfy all the demands of her whole being? You may paint her in poetry or fiction, as a frail vine, clinging to her brother man for support, and dying when deprived of it; and all this may sound well enough to please the imaginations of school-girls, or love-lorn maidens.

But woman—the true woman—if you would render her happy, it needs more than the mere development of her affectional nature. Her conscience should be enlightened, her faith in the true and right established, scope given to her Heaven-endowed and God-given faculties.

The true aim of female education should be not a development of one or two, but all the faculties of the human soul, because no perfect womanhood is developed by imperfect culture. Intense love is often akin to intense suffering, and to trust the whole wealth of a woman's nature on the frail bark of human love, may often be like trusting a cargo of gold and precious gems, to a bark that has never battled with the storm, or buffeted the waves.

Is it any wonder, then, that so many life-barks go down, paving the ocean of time with precious hearts and wasted hopes? that so many float around us, shattered and dismasted wrecks? that so many are stranded on the shoals of existence, mournful beacons and solemn warnings for the thoughtless, to whom marriage is a careless and hasty rushing together of the affections?

Alas that an institution so fraught with good for humanity should be so perverted, and that state of life, which should be filled with happiness, become so replete with misery.

And this was the fate of Laura Lagrange. For a brief period after her marriage her life seemed like a bright and beautiful dream, full of hope and radiant with joy. And then there came a change—he found other attractions that lay beyond the pale of home influences.

The gambling saloon had power to win him from her side, he had lived in an element of unhealthy and unhallowed excitements, and the society of a loving wife, the pleasures of a well-regulated home, were enjoyments too tame for one who had vitiated his tastes by the pleasures of sin.

There were charmed houses of vice, built upon dead men's loves, where, amid the flow of song, laughter, wine, and careless mirth, he would spend hour after hour, forgetting the cheek that was paling through his neglect, heedless of the tear-dimmed eyes, peering anxiously into the darkness, waiting, or watching his return.

The influence of old associations was upon

him. In early life, home had been to him a place of ceilings and walls, not a true home, built upon goodness, love and truth. It was a place where velvet carpets hushed its tread, where images of loveliness and beauty invoked into being by painter's art and sculptor's skill, pleased the eye and gratified the taste, where magnificence surrounded his way and costly clothing adorned his person; but it was not the place for the true culture and right development of his soul.

His father had been too much engrossed in making money, and his mother in spending it, in striving to maintain a fashionable position in society, and shining in the eyes of the world, to give the proper direction to the character of their wayward and impulsive son. His mother put beautiful robes upon his body, but left ugly scars upon his soul; she pampered his appetite, but starved his spirit.

Every mother should be a true artist, who knows how to weave into her child's life images of grace and beauty, the true poet capable of writing on the soul of childhood the harmony of love and truth, and teaching it how to produce the grandest of all poems—the poetry of a true and noble life.

But in his home, a love for the good, the true and right, had been sacrificed at the shrine of frivolity and fashion. That parental authority which should have been preserved as a string of precious pearls, unbroken and unscattered, was simply the administration of chance.

At one time obedience was enforced by authority, at another time by flattery and promises, and just as often it was not enforced at all. His early associations were formed as chance directed, and from his want of home-training, his character received a bias, his life a shade, which ran through every avenue of his existence, and darkened all his future hours.

Oh, if we would trace the history of all the crimes that have o'ershadowed this sin-shrouded and sorrow-darkened world of ours, how many might be seen arising from the wrong home influences, or the weakening of the home ties.

Home should always be the best school for the affections, the birthplace of high resolves, and the altar upon which lofty aspirations are kindled, from whence the soul may go forth strengthened, to act its part aright in the great drama of life with conscience enlightened, affections cultivated, and reason and judgment dominant.

But alas for the young wife. Her husband had not been blessed with such a home. When he entered the arena of life, the voices from home did not linger around his path as angels of guidance about his steps; they were not like so many messages to invite him to deeds of high and holy worth.

The memory of no sainted mother arose

between him and deeds of darkness; the earnest prayers of no father arrested him in his downward course: and before a year of his married life had waned, his young wife had learned to wait and mourn his frequent and uncalled-for absence.

More than once had she seen him come home from his midnight haunts, the bright intelligence of his eye displaced by the drunkard's stare, and his manly gait changed to the inebriate's* stagger; and she was beginning to know the bitter agony that is compressed in the mournful words, a drunkard's wife.

And then there came a bright but brief episode in her experience; the angel of life gave to her existence a deeper meaning and loftier significance; she sheltered in the warm clasp of her loving arms, a dear babe, a precious child, whose love filled every chamber of her heart, and felt the fount of maternal love gushing so new within her soul. That child was hers.

How overshadowing was the love with which she bent over its helplessness, how much it helped to fill the void and chasms in her soul. How many lonely hours were beguiled by its winsome ways, its answering smiles and fond caresses. How exquisite and solemn was the feeling that thrilled her heart when she clasped the tiny hands together and taught her dear child to call God "Our Father."

What a blessing was that child. The father paused in his headlong career, awed by the strange beauty and precocious intellect of his child; and the mother's life had a better expression through her ministrations of love. And then there came hours of bitter anguish, shading the sunlight of her home and hushing the music of her heart.

The angel of death bent over the couch of her child and beaconed it away. Closer and closer the mother strained her child to her wildly heaving breast, and struggled with the heavy hand that lay upon its heart. Love and agony contended with death, and the language of the mother's heart was,

'Oh, Death, away! that innocent is mine;
I cannot spare him from my arms
To lay him, Death, in thine.
I am a mother, Death; I gave that darling birth
I could not bear his lifeless limbs
Should moulder in the earth.'

But death was stronger than love and mightier than agony and won the child for the land of crystal founts and deathless flowers, and the poor, stricken mother sat down beneath the shadow of her mighty grief, feeling as if a great light had gone out from her soul, and that the sunshine had suddenly faded around her path. She turned in her deep anguish to the father of her child, the loved and cherished dead.

For a while his words were kind and tender, his heart seemed subdued, and his tenderness fell upon her worn and weary heart like rain on perishing flowers, or cooling waters to lips all parched with thirst and scorched with fever; but the change was evanescent,* the influence of unhallowed associations and evil habits had vitiated and poisoned the springs of his existence.

They had bound him in their meshes, and he lacked the moral strength to break his fetters, and stand erect in all the strength and dignity of a true manhood, making life's highest excellence his ideal, and striving to gain it.

And yet moments of deep contrition* would sweep over him, when he would resolve to abandon the wine-cup forever, when he was ready to forswear the handling of another card, and he would try to break away from the associations that he felt were working his ruin; but when the hour of temptation came his strength was weakness, his earnest purposes were cobwebs, his well meant resolutions ropes of sand, and thus passed year after year of the married life of Laura Lagrange.

She tried to hide her agony from the public gaze, to smile when her heart was almost breaking. But year after year her voice grew fainter and sadder, her once light and bounding step grew slower and faltering. Year after year she wrestled with agony, and strove with despair, till the quick eyes of her brother read, in the paling of her cheek and the dimming eye, the secret anguish of her worn and weary spirit. On that wan, sad face, he saw the death-tokens, and he knew the dark wing of the mystic angel swept coldly around her path.

'Laura,' said her brother to her one day, 'you are not well, and I think you need our mother's tender care and nursing. You are daily losing strength, and if you will go I will accompany you.' At first, she hesitated, she shrank almost instinctively from presenting that pale sad face to the loved ones at home. That face was such a telltale; it told of heart-sickness, of hope deferred, and the mournful story of unrequited love.

But then a deep yearning for home sympathy woke within her a passionate longing for love's kind words, for tenderness and heart support, and she resolved to seek the home of her childhood and lay her weary head upon her mother's bosom, to be folded again in her loving arms, to lay that poor, bruised and aching heart where it might beat and throb closely to the loved ones at home.

A kind welcome awaited her. All that love and tenderness could devise was done to bring the bloom to her cheek and the light to her eye; but it was all in vain; her's was a disease that no medicine could cure, no earthly balm would heal. It was a slow wasting of the vital forces, the sickness of the soul. The unkindness and neglect of her husband, lay like a leaden weight upon her heart, and slowly oozed way its life-drops.

And where was he that had won her love, and then cast it aside as a useless thing, who rifled her heart of its wealth and spread bitter ashes upon its broken altars? He was lingering away from her when the death-damps were gathering on her brow, when his name was trembling on her lips! lingering away! when she was watching his coming, though the death films were gathering before her eyes, and earthly things were fading from her vision.

'I think I hear him now,' said the dying woman, 'surely that is his step;' but the sound died away in the distance. Again she started from an uneasy slumber, 'that is his voice! I am so glad he has come.'

Tears gathered in the eyes of the sad watchers by that dying bed, for they knew that she was deceived. He had not returned. For her sake they wished his coming. Slowly the hours waned away, and then came the sad, soul-sickening thought that she was forgotten, forgotten in the last hour of human need, forgotten when the spirit, about to be dissolved, paused for the last time on the threshold of existence, a weary watcher at the gates of death.

'He has forgotten me,' again she faintly murmured, and the last tears she would ever shed on earth sprung to her mournful eyes, and clasping her hands together in silent anguish, a few broken sentences issued from her pale and quivering lips. They were prayers for strength and earnest pleading for him who had desolated her young life, by turning its sunshine to shadows, its smiles to tears.

'He has forgotten me,' she murmured again, 'but I can bear it, the bitterness of death is passed, and soon I hope to exchange the shadows of death for the brightness of eternity, the rugged paths of life for the golden streets of glory, and the care and turmoils of earth for the peace and rest of heaven.'

Her voice grew fainter and fainter, they saw the shadows that never deceive flit* over her pale and faded face, and knew that the death angel waited to soothe their weary one to rest, to calm the throbbing of her bosom and cool the fever of her brain.

And amid the silent hush of their grief the freed spirit, refined through suffering, and brought into divine harmony through the spirit of the living Christ, passed over the dark waters of death as on a bridge of light, over whose radiant arches hovering angels bent. They parted the dark locks from her marble brow, closed the waxen lids over the once bright and laughing eye, and left her to the dreamless slumber of the grave.

Her cousin turned from that death-bed a sadder and wiser woman. She resolved more earnestly than ever to make the world better by her example, gladder by her presence, and to kindle the fires of her genius on the altars of universal love and truth. She had a higher and better object in all her writings than the mere acquisition of gold, or acquirement of fame.

She felt that she had a high and holy mission on the battle-field of existence, that life was not given her to be frittered* away in nonsense, or wasted away in trifling pursuits. She would willingly espouse an unpopular cause but not an unrighteous one. In her the down-trodden slave found an earnest advocate; the flying fugitive remembered her kindness as he stepped cautiously through our Republic, to gain his freedom in a monarchial land, having broken the chains on which the rust of centuries had gathered.

Little children learned to name her with affection, the poor called her blessed, as she broke her bread to the pale lips of hunger. Her life was like a beautiful story, only it was clothed with the dignity of reality and invested with the sublimity of truth. True, she was an old maid.

No husband brightened her life with his love, or shaded it with his neglect. No children nestling lovingly in her arms called her mother. No one appended Mrs to her name; she was indeed an old maid, not vainly striving to keep up an appearance of girlishness, when departed was written on her youth.

Not vainly pining at her loneliness and isolation: the world was full of warm, loving hearts, and her own beat in unison with them. Neither was she always sentimentally sighing for something to love, objects of affection were all around her, and the world was not so wealthy in love that it had no use for her's; in blessing others she made a life and benediction, and as old age descended peacefully and gently upon her, she had learned one of life's most precious lessons, that true happiness consists not so much in the fruition of our wishes as in the regulation of desires and the full development and right culture of our whole statures.

If you liked reading this story, you must also read:

Minnie's Sacrifice, Iola Leroy, or Shadows Uplifted, Light Beyond the Darkness

---

GLOSSARY:

Abolitionist: A person who favours the removal of a practice or institution, usually refers to the anti-slavery cause

Suffragist: A person advocating that the right to vote be extended to more people, especially to women

Affinity: Sympathy or a natural liking for and understanding of someone or something

Auspices: A divine or prophetic token

Sepulchre: A small room or monument, cut in rock or built of stone, in which a dead person is laid or buried

Eloquence: Fluent or persuasive speaking or writing

Inebriate: Drunk or intoxicated

Evanescent: Vanishing or fading

Contrition: The state of feeling remorse

Flit: Move swiftly and lightly

Frittered: To waste time, money, or energy on trifling matters

Katherine Mansfield, New Zealand

(October 14, 1888 – January 9, 1923)

Katherine Mansfield, the renowned New Zealand writer, had an innovative, accessible, and psychologically acute approach to short stories that led her to pioneer the shape of short stories in the twentieth century.

Kathleen Mansfield Murry was nineteen when she completed her education and left New Zealand to establish herself as a writer. Mansfield was gripped by London and quickly fell into a bohemian* lifestyle. Mansfield began work on her first collection of stories, *In a German Pension* (1911), which contains her early disillusion* of the world through witty tales. She also befriended the literary genius, Virginia Woolf and DH Lawrence in this period.

When her brother died she wrote *Prelude* (1918), a collection of short stories that brilliantly evoked her family's recollections of New Zealand. Mansfield produced her best work with *Bliss* (1920) and *The Garden Party* (1922) that carried a nuanced depiction of genteel* frustration. She passed away from tuberculosis in 1923.

She wrote about the difficulties and vulnerabilities of close-knit family relationships. Even though she depicts the social consequences of war, her writings still manage to bring out the beauty and vitality that can be found in the mundane and difficult experiences of life. Her evolved and distinctive prose style with overtones of poetry makes her work revolutionary. Her work continues to have an enormous influence on the development of the short story as a form of literature. She will always be known as one of the pioneers of twentieth-century short story writing.

The Garden Party

And after all the weather was ideal. They could not have had a more perfect day for a garden-party if they had ordered it. Windless, warm, the sky without a cloud. Only the blue was veiled with a haze of light gold, as it is sometimes in early summer. The gardener had been up since dawn, mowing the lawns and sweeping them, until the grass and the dark flat rosettes where the daisy plants had been seemed to shine. As for the roses, you could not help feeling they understood that roses are the only flowers that impress people at garden-parties; the only flowers that everybody is certain of knowing. Hundreds, yes, literally hundreds, had come out in a single night; the green bushes bowed down as though they had been visited by archangels.*

Breakfast was not yet over before the men came to put up the marquee.*

'Where do you want the marquee put, mother?'

'My dear child, it's no use asking me. I'm determined to leave everything to you children this year. Forget I am your mother. Treat me as an honoured guest.'

But Meg could not possibly go and supervise the men. She had washed her hair before breakfast, and she sat drinking her coffee in a green turban, with a dark wet curl stamped on each cheek. Jose, the butterfly, always came down in a silk petticoat and a kimono jacket.

'You'll have to go, Laura; you're the artistic one.'

Away Laura flew, still holding her piece of bread-and-butter. It's so delicious to have an excuse for eating out of doors, and besides, she loved having to arrange things; she always felt she could do it so much better than anybody else.

Four men in their shirt-sleeves stood grouped together on the garden path. They carried staves covered with rolls of canvas, and they had big tool-bags slung on their backs. They looked impressive. Laura wished now that she had not got the bread-and-butter, but there was nowhere to put it, and she couldn't possibly throw it away. She blushed and tried to look severe and even a little bit short-sighted as she came up to them.

'Good morning,' she said, copying her mother's voice. But that sounded so fearfully affected that she was ashamed, and stammered like a little girl, 'Oh—er—have you come—is it about the marquee?'

'That's right, miss,' said the tallest of the men, a lanky, freckled fellow, and he shifted his tool-bag, knocked back his straw hat and smiled down at her. 'That's about it.'

His smile was so easy, so friendly that Laura recovered. What nice eyes he had, small, but such a dark blue! And now she looked at the others, they were smiling too. 'Cheer up, we won't bite,' their smile seemed to say. How very nice workmen were! And what a beautiful morning! She mustn't mention the morning; she must be business-like. The marquee.

'Well, what about the lily-lawn? Would that do?'

And she pointed to the lily-lawn with the hand that didn't hold the bread-and-butter. They turned, they stared in the direction. A little fat chap thrust out his under-lip, and the tall fellow frowned.

'I don't fancy it,' said he. 'Not conspicuous enough. You see, with a thing like a marquee,' and he turned to Laura in his easy way, 'you want to put it somewhere where it'll give you a bang slap in the eye, if you follow me.'

Laura's upbringing made her wonder for

a moment whether it was quite respectful of a workman to talk to her of bangs slap in the eye. But she did quite follow him.

'A corner of the tennis-court,' she suggested. 'But the band's going to be in one corner.'

'H'm, going to have a band, are you?' said another of the workmen. He was pale. He had a haggard look as his dark eyes scanned the tennis-court. What was he thinking?

'Only a very small band,' said Laura gently. Perhaps he wouldn't mind so much if the band was quite small. But the tall fellow interrupted.

'Look here, miss, that's the place. Against those trees. Over there. That'll do fine.'

Against the karakas. Then the karaka-trees would be hidden. And they were so lovely, with their broad, gleaming leaves, and their clusters of yellow fruit. They were like trees you imagined growing on a desert island, proud, solitary, lifting their leaves and fruits to the sun in a kind of silent splendour. Must they be hidden by a marquee?

They must. Already the men had shouldered their staves* and were making for the place. Only the tall fellow was left. He bent down, pinched a sprig of lavender, put his thumb and forefinger to his nose and snuffed up the smell. When Laura saw that gesture she forgot all about the karakas in her wonder at him caring for things like that—caring for the smell of lavender. How many men that she knew would have done such a thing? Oh, how extraordinarily nice workmen were, she thought. Why couldn't she have workmen for her friends rather than the silly boys she danced with and who came to Sunday night supper? She would get on much better with men like these.

It's all the fault, she decided, as the tall fellow drew something on the back of an envelope, something that was to be looped up or left to hang, of these absurd class distinctions. Well, for her part, she didn't feel them. Not a bit, not an atom. ... And now there came the chock-chock of wooden hammers. Some one whistled, some one sang out, 'Are you right there, matey?' 'Matey!' The friendliness of it, the—the—Just to prove how happy she was, just to show the tall fellow how at home she felt, and how she despised stupid conventions, Laura took a big bite of her bread-and-butter as she stared at the little drawing. She felt just like a work-girl.

'Laura, Laura, where are you? Telephone, Laura!' a voice cried from the house.

'Coming!' Away she skimmed, over the lawn, up the path, up the steps, across the veranda, and into the porch. In the hall her father and Laurie were brushing their hats ready to go to the office.

'I say, Laura,' said Laurie very fast, 'you might just give a squiz at my coat before this afternoon. See if it wants pressing.'

'I will,' said she. Suddenly she couldn't stop herself. She ran at Laurie and gave him a small, quick squeeze. 'Oh, I do love parties, don't you?' gasped Laura.

'Ra-ther,' said Laurie's warm, boyish voice, and he squeezed his sister too, and gave her a gentle push. 'Dash off to the telephone, old girl.'

The telephone. 'Yes, yes; oh yes. Kitty? Good morning, dear. Come to lunch? Do, dear. Delighted of course. It will only be a very scratch meal—just the sandwich crusts and broken meringue-shells and what's left over. Yes, isn't it a perfect morning? Your white? Oh, I certainly should. One moment—hold the line. Mother's calling.' And Laura sat back. 'What, mother? Can't hear.'

Mrs Sheridan's voice floated down the stairs. 'Tell her to wear that sweet hat she had on last Sunday.'

'Mother says you're to wear that sweet hat you had on last Sunday. Good. One o'clock. Bye-bye.'

Laura put back the receiver, flung her arms over her head, took a deep breath, stretched and let them fall. 'Huh,' she sighed, and the moment after the sigh she sat up quickly. She was still, listening. All the doors in the house seemed to be open. The house was alive with soft, quick steps and running voices. The green baize* door that led to the kitchen regions swung open and shut with a muffled thud. And now there came a long, chuckling absurd sound. It was the heavy piano being moved on its stiff castors. But the air! If you stopped to notice, was the air always like this? Little faint winds were playing chase, in at the tops of the windows, out at the doors. And there were two tiny spots of sun, one on the inkpot, one on a silver photograph frame, playing too. Darling little spots. Especially the one on the inkpot lid. It was quite warm. A warm little silver star. She could have kissed it.

The front door bell pealed, and there sounded the rustle of Sadie's print skirt on the stairs. A man's voice murmured; Sadie answered, careless, 'I'm sure I don't know. Wait. I'll ask Mrs Sheridan.'

'What is it, Sadie?' Laura came into the hall.

'It's the florist, Miss Laura.'

It was, indeed. There, just inside the door, stood a wide, shallow tray full of pots of pink lilies. No other kind. Nothing but lilies—canna lilies, big pink flowers, wide open, radiant, almost frighteningly alive on bright crimson stems.

'O-oh, Sadie!' said Laura, and the sound was like a little moan. She crouched down as if to warm herself at that blaze of lilies; she felt they were in her fingers, on her lips, growing in her breast.

'It's some mistake,' she said faintly. 'Nobody ever ordered so many. Sadie, go and find mother.'

But at that moment Mrs Sheridan joined them.

'It's quite right,' she said calmly. 'Yes, I ordered them. Aren't they lovely?' She pressed Laura's arm. 'I was passing the shop yesterday, and I saw them in the window. And I suddenly thought for once in my life I shall have enough canna lilies. The garden-party will be a good excuse.'

'But I thought you said you didn't mean to interfere,' said Laura. Sadie had gone. The florist's man was still outside at his van. She put her arm round her mother's neck and gently, very gently, she bit her mother's ear.

'My darling child, you wouldn't like a logical mother, would you? Don't do that. Here's the man.'

He carried more lilies still, another whole tray.

'Bank them up, just inside the door, on both sides of the porch, please,' said Mrs Sheridan. 'Don't you agree, Laura?'

'Oh, I do, mother.'

In the drawing-room Meg, Jose and good little Hans had at last succeeded in moving the piano.

'Now, if we put this chesterfield against the wall and move everything out of the room except the chairs, don't you think?'

'Quite.'

'Hans, move these tables into the smoking-room, and bring a sweeper to take these marks off the carpet and—one moment, Hans—' Jose loved giving orders to the servants, and they loved obeying her. She always made them feel they were taking part in some drama. 'Tell mother and Miss Laura to come here at once.'

'Very good, Miss Jose.'

She turned to Meg. 'I want to hear what the piano sounds like, just in case I'm asked to sing this afternoon. Let's try over "This life is Weary."'

Pom! Ta-ta-ta Tee-ta! The piano burst out so passionately that Jose's face changed. She clasped her hands. She looked mournfully and enigmatically at her mother and Laura as they came in.

This Life is Wee-ary,
A Tear—a Sigh.
A Love that Chan-ges,
This Life is Wee-ary,
A Tear—a Sigh.
A Love that Chan-ges,
And then ... Good-bye!

But at the word 'Good-bye,' and although the piano sounded more desperate than ever, her face broke into a brilliant, dreadfully unsympathetic smile.

'Aren't I in good voice, mummy?' she beamed.

This Life is Wee-ary,
Hope comes to Die.
A Dream—a Wa-kening.

But now Sadie interrupted them. 'What is it, Sadie?'

'If you please, m'm, cook says have you got the

flags for the sandwiches?'

'The flags for the sandwiches, Sadie?' echoed Mrs Sheridan dreamily. And the children knew by her face that she hadn't got them. 'Let me see.' And she said to Sadie firmly, 'Tell cook I'll let her have them in ten minutes.'

Sadie went.

'Now, Laura,' said her mother quickly, 'come with me into the smoking-room. I've got the names somewhere on the back of an envelope. You'll have to write them out for me. Meg, go upstairs this minute and take that wet thing off your head. Jose, run and finish dressing this instant. Do you hear me, children, or shall I have to tell your father when he comes home to-night? And—and, Jose, pacify cook if you do go into the kitchen, will you? I'm terrified of her this morning.'

The envelope was found at last behind the dining-room clock, though how it had got there Mrs Sheridan could not imagine.

'One of you children must have stolen it out of my bag, because I remember vividly-cream-cheese and lemon-curd. Have you done that?'

'Yes.'

'Egg and—' Mrs Sheridan held the envelope away from her. 'It looks like mice. It can't be mice, can it?'

'Olive, pet,' said Laura, looking over her shoulder.

'Yes, of course, olive. What a horrible combination it sounds. Egg and olive.'

They were finished at last, and Laura took them off to the kitchen. She found Jose there pacifying the cook, who did not look at all terrifying.

'I have never seen such exquisite sandwiches,' said Jose's rapturous voice. 'How many kinds did you say there were, cook? Fifteen?'

'Fifteen, Miss Jose.'

'Well, cook, I congratulate you.'

Cook swept up crusts with the long sandwich knife, and smiled broadly.

'Godber's has come,' announced Sadie, issuing out of the pantry. She had seen the man pass the window.

That meant the cream puffs had come. Godber's were famous for their cream puffs. Nobody ever thought of making them at home.

'Bring them in and put them on the table, my girl,' ordered cook.

Sadie brought them in and went back to the door. Of course Laura and Jose were far too grown-up to really care about such things. All the same, they couldn't help agreeing that the puffs looked very attractive. Very. Cook began arranging them, shaking off the extra icing sugar.

'Don't they carry one back to all one's parties?' said Laura.

'I suppose they do,' said practical Jose,

who never liked to be carried back. 'They look beautifully light and feathery, I must say.'

'Have one each, my dears,' said cook in her comfortable voice. 'Yer ma won't know.'

Oh, impossible. Fancy cream puffs so soon after breakfast. The very idea made one shudder. All the same, two minutes later Jose and Laura were licking their fingers with that absorbed inward look that only comes from whipped cream.

'Let's go into the garden, out by the back way,' suggested Laura. 'I want to see how the men are getting on with the marquee. They're such awfully nice men.'

But the back door was blocked by cook, Sadie, Godber's man and Hans.

Something had happened.

'Tuk-tuk-tuk,' clucked cook like an agitated hen. Sadie had her hand clapped to her cheek as though she had toothache. Hans's face was screwed up in the effort to understand. Only Godber's man seemed to be enjoying himself; it was his story.

'What's the matter? What's happened?'

'There's been a horrible accident,' said Cook. 'A man killed.'

'A man killed! Where? How? When?'

But Godber's man wasn't going to have his story snatched from under his very nose.

'Know those little cottages just below here, miss?' Know them? Of course, she knew them.

'Well, there's a young chap living there, name of Scott, a carter. His horse shied at a traction-engine, corner of Hawke Street this morning, and he was thrown out on the back of his head. Killed.'

'Dead!' Laura stared at Godber's man.

'Dead when they picked him up,' said Godber's man with relish. 'They were taking the body home as I come up here.' And he said to the cook, 'He's left a wife and five little ones.'

'Jose, come here.' Laura caught hold of her sister's sleeve and dragged her through the kitchen to the other side of the green baize door. There she paused and leaned against it. 'Jose!' she said, horrified, 'however are we going to stop everything?'

'Stop everything, Laura!' cried Jose in astonishment. 'What do you mean?'

'Stop the garden-party, of course.' Why did Jose pretend?

But Jose was still more amazed. 'Stop the garden-party? My dear Laura, don't be so absurd. Of course we can't do anything of the kind. Nobody expects us to. Don't be so extravagant.'

'But we can't possibly have a garden-party with a man dead just outside the front gate.'

That really was extravagant, for the little cottages were in a lane to themselves at the very bottom of a steep rise that led up to the house. A broad road ran between. True, they were far too near. They were the greatest possible eyesore, and they had no right to be in that neighbourhood at all. They were little mean dwellings painted a chocolate brown. In the garden patches there was nothing but cabbage stalks, sick hens and tomato cans. The very smoke coming out of their chimneys was poverty-stricken. Little rags and shreds of smoke, so unlike the great silvery plumes that uncurled from the Sheridans' chimneys. Washerwomen lived in the lane and sweeps and a cobbler, and a man whose house-front was studded all over with minute bird-cages. Children swarmed. When the Sheridans were little they were forbidden to set foot there because of the revolting language and of what they might catch. But since they were grown up, Laura and Laurie on their prowls sometimes walked through. It was disgusting and sordid.* They came out with a shudder. But still one must go everywhere; one must see everything. So through they went.

'And just think of what the band would sound like to that poor woman,' said Laura.

'Oh, Laura!' Jose began to be seriously annoyed. 'If you're going to stop a band playing every time some one has an accident, you'll lead a very strenuous life. I'm every bit as sorry about it as you. I feel just as sympathetic.' Her eyes hardened. She looked at her sister just as she used to when they were little and fighting together. 'You won't bring a drunken workman back to life by being sentimental,' she said softly.

'Drunk! Who said he was drunk?' Laura turned furiously on Jose. She said, just as they had used to say on those occasions, 'I'm going straight up to tell mother.'

'Do, dear,' cooed Jose.

'Mother, can I come into your room?' Laura turned the big glass door-knob.

'Of course, child. Why, what's the matter? What's given you such a colour?' And Mrs Sheridan turned round from her dressing-table. She was trying on a new hat.

'Mother, a man's been killed,' began Laura.

'Not in the garden?' interrupted her mother.

'No, no!'

'Oh, what a fright you gave me!' Mrs Sheridan sighed with relief, and took off the big hat and held it on her knees.

'But listen, mother,' said Laura. Breathless, half-choking, she told the dreadful story. 'Of course, we can't have our party, can we?' she pleaded. 'The band and everybody arriving. They'd hear us, mother; they're nearly neighbours!'

To Laura's astonishment her mother behaved just like Jose; it was harder to bear because she seemed amused. She refused to take Laura seriously.

'But, my dear child, use your common sense. It's only by accident we've heard of it. If some one had died there normally—and I can't understand how they keep alive in those poky little holes—we should still be having our party, shouldn't we?'

Laura had to say 'yes' to that, but she felt it was all wrong. She sat down on her mother's sofa and pinched the cushion frill.

'Mother, isn't it terribly heartless of us?' she asked.

'Darling!' Mrs Sheridan got up and came over to her, carrying the hat. Before Laura could stop her she had popped it on. 'My child!' said her mother, 'the hat is yours. It's made for you. It's much too young for me. I have never seen you look such a picture. Look at yourself!' And she held up her hand-mirror.

'But, mother,' Laura began again. She couldn't look at herself; she turned aside.

This time Mrs Sheridan lost patience just as Jose had done.

'You are being very absurd, Laura,' she said coldly. 'People like that don't expect sacrifices from us. And it's not very sympathetic to spoil everybody's enjoyment as you're doing now.'

'I don't understand,' said Laura, and she walked quickly out of the room into her own bedroom. There, quite by chance, the first thing she saw was this charming girl in the mirror, in her black hat trimmed with gold daisies, and a long black velvet ribbon. Never had she imagined she could look like that. Is mother right? she thought. And now she hoped her mother was right. Am I being extravagant? Perhaps it was extravagant. Just for a moment she had another glimpse of that poor woman and those little children, and the body being carried into the house. But it all seemed blurred, unreal, like a picture in the newspaper. I'll remember it again after the party's over, she decided. And somehow that seemed quite the best plan....

Lunch was over by half-past one. By half-past two they were all ready for the fray. The green-coated band had arrived and was established in a corner of the tennis-court.

'My dear!' trilled Kitty Maitland, 'aren't they too like frogs for words? You ought to have arranged them round the pond with the conductor in the middle on a leaf.'

Laurie arrived and hailed them on his way to dress. At the sight of him Laura remembered the accident again. She wanted to tell him. If Laurie agreed with the others, then it was bound to be all right. And she followed him into the hall.

'Laurie!'

'Hallo!' He was half-way upstairs, but when he turned round and saw Laura he suddenly puffed out his cheeks and goggled his eyes at her. 'My word, Laura! You do look stunning,' said Laurie. 'What an absolutely topping hat!'

Laura said faintly 'Is it?' and smiled up at Laurie, and didn't tell him after all.

Soon after that people began coming in streams. The band struck up; the hired waiters ran from the house to the marquee. Wherever you looked there were couples strolling, bending to the flowers, greeting, moving on over the lawn. They were like bright birds that had alighted in the Sheridans' garden for this one afternoon, on their way to—where? Ah, what happiness it is to be with people who all are happy, to press hands, press cheeks, smile into eyes.

'Darling Laura, how well you look!'

'What a becoming hat, child!'

'Laura, you look quite Spanish. I've never seen you look so striking.'

And Laura, glowing, answered softly, 'Have you had tea? Won't you have an ice? The passion-fruit ices really are rather special.' She ran to her father and begged him. 'Daddy darling, can't the band have something to drink?'

And the perfect afternoon slowly ripened, slowly faded, slowly its petals closed.

'Never a more delightful garden-party. ... ' 'The greatest success. ... ' 'Quite the most. ... '

Laura helped her mother with the good-byes. They stood side by side in the porch till it was all over.

'All over, all over, thank heaven,' said Mrs Sheridan. 'Round up the others, Laura. Let's go and have some fresh coffee. I'm exhausted. Yes, it's been very successful. But oh, these parties, these parties! Why will you children insist on giving parties!' And they all of them sat down in the deserted marquee.

'Have a sandwich, daddy dear. I wrote the flag.'

'Thanks.' Mr Sheridan took a bite and the sandwich was gone. He took another. 'I suppose you didn't hear of a beastly accident that happened to-day?' he said.

'My dear,' said Mrs Sheridan, holding up her hand, 'we did. It nearly ruined the party. Laura insisted we should put it off.'

'Oh, mother!' Laura didn't want to be teased about it.

'It was a horrible affair all the same,' said Mr Sheridan. 'The chap was married too. Lived just below in the lane, and leaves a wife and half a dozen kiddies, so they say.'

An awkward little silence fell. Mrs Sheridan fidgeted with her cup. Really, it was very tactless of father. ...

Suddenly she looked up. There on the table were all those sandwiches, cakes, puffs, all uneaten, all going to be wasted. She had one of her brilliant ideas.

'I know,' she said. 'Let's make up a basket. Let's send that poor creature some of this perfectly good food. At any rate, it will be the greatest treat for the children. Don't you agree? And she's sure to have neighbours calling in and so on. What a point to have it all ready prepared. Laura!' She jumped up. 'Get me the big basket out of the stairs cupboard.'

'But, mother, do you really think it's a good idea?' said Laura.

Again, how curious, she seemed to be different from them all. To take scraps from their party. Would the poor woman really like that?

'Of course! What's the matter with you to-day? An hour or two ago you were insisting on us being sympathetic, and now—'

Oh well! Laura ran for the basket. It was filled, it was heaped by her mother.

'Take it yourself, darling,' said she. 'Run down just as you are. No, wait, take the arum lilies too. People of that class are so impressed by arum lilies.'

'The stems will ruin her lace frock,' said practical Jose.

So they would. Just in time. 'Only the basket, then. And, Laura!' her mother followed her out of the marquee—'don't on any account—'

'What mother?'

No, better not put such ideas into the child's head! 'Nothing! Run along.'

It was just growing dusky as Laura shut their garden gates. A big dog ran by like a shadow. The road gleamed white, and down below in the hollow the little cottages were in deep shade. How quiet it seemed after the afternoon. Here she was going down the hill to somewhere where a man lay dead, and she couldn't realize it. Why couldn't she? She stopped a minute. And it seemed to her that kisses, voices, tinkling spoons, laughter, the smell of crushed grass were somehow inside her. She had no room for anything else. How strange! She looked up at the pale sky, and all she thought was, 'Yes, it was the most successful party.'

Now the broad road was crossed. The lane began, smoky and dark. Women in shawls and men's tweed caps hurried by. Men hung over the palings; the children played in the doorways. A low hum came from the mean little cottages. In some of them there was a flicker of light, and a shadow, crab-like, moved across the window. Laura bent her head and hurried on. She wished now she had put on a coat. How her frock shone! And the big hat with the velvet streamer—if only it was another hat! Were the people looking at her? They must be. It was a mistake to have come; she knew all along it was a mistake. Should she go back even now?

No, too late. This was the house. It must be. A dark knot of people stood outside. Beside the gate an old, old woman with a crutch sat in a chair, watching. She had her feet on a newspaper. The voices stopped as Laura drew near. The group parted. It was as though she was expected, as though they had known she was coming here.

Laura was terribly nervous. Tossing the velvet

ribbon over her shoulder, she said to a woman standing by, 'Is this Mrs Scott's house?' and the woman, smiling queerly, said, 'It is, my lass.'

Oh, to be away from this! She actually said, 'Help me, God,' as she walked up the tiny path and knocked. To be away from those staring eyes, or to be covered up in anything, one of those women's shawls even. I'll just leave the basket and go, she decided. I shan't even wait for it to be emptied.

Then the door opened. A little woman in black showed in the gloom.

Laura said, 'Are you Mrs Scott?' But to her horror the woman answered, 'Walk in please, miss,' and she was shut in the passage.

'No,' said Laura, 'I don't want to come in. I only want to leave this basket. Mother sent—'

The little woman in the gloomy passage seemed not to have heard her. 'Step this way, please, miss,' she said in an oily voice, and Laura followed her.

She found herself in a wretched little low kitchen, lighted by a smoky lamp. There was a woman sitting before the fire.

'Em,' said the little creature who had let her in. 'Em! It's a young lady.' She turned to Laura. She said meaningly, 'I'm 'er sister, miss. You'll excuse 'er, won't you?'

'Oh, but of course!' said Laura. 'Please, please don't disturb her. I—I only want to leave—'

But at that moment the woman at the fire

turned round. Her face, puffed up, red, with swollen eyes and swollen lips, looked terrible. She seemed as though she couldn't understand why Laura was there. What did it mean? Why was this stranger standing in the kitchen with a basket? What was it all about? And the poor face puckered up again.

'All right, my dear,' said the other. 'I'll thenk the young lady.'

And again she began, 'You'll excuse her, miss, I'm sure,' and her face, swollen too, tried an oily smile.

Laura only wanted to get out, to get away. She was back in the passage. The door opened. She walked straight through into the bedroom, where the dead man was lying.

'You'd like a look at 'im, wouldn't you?' said Em's sister, and she brushed past Laura over to the bed. 'Don't be afraid, my lass,'—and now her voice sounded fond and sly, and fondly she drew down the sheet—"e looks a picture. There's nothing to show. Come along, my dear.'

Laura came.

There lay a young man, fast asleep—sleeping so soundly, so deeply, that he was far, far away from them both. Oh, so remote, so peaceful. He was dreaming. Never wake him up again. His head was sunk in the pillow, his eyes were closed; they were blind under the closed eyelids. He was given up to his dream. What did garden-parties and baskets and lace frocks matter to him? He was far from all those things. He was wonderful, beautiful. While they were laughing and while the band was playing, this marvel had come to the lane. Happy... happy. ... All is well, said that sleeping face. This is just as it should be. I am content.

But all the same you had to cry, and she couldn't go out of the room without saying something to him. Laura gave a loud childish sob.

'Forgive my hat,' she said.

And this time she didn't wait for Em's sister. She found her way out of the door, down the path, past all those dark people. At the corner of the lane she met Laurie.

He stepped out of the shadow. 'Is that you, Laura?'

'Yes.'

'Mother was getting anxious. Was it all right?'

'Yes, quite. Oh, Laurie!' She took his arm, she pressed up against him.

'I say, you're not crying, are you?' asked her brother.

Laura shook her head. She was.

Laurie put his arm round her shoulder. 'Don't cry,' he said in his warm, loving voice. 'Was it awful?'

'No,' sobbed Laura. 'It was simply marvellous. But Laurie—' She stopped, she looked at her brother. 'Isn't life,' she stammered, 'isn't life—' But what life was she couldn't explain. No matter. He quite understood.

'Isn't it, darling?' said Laurie.

If you liked reading this story, you must also read:

The Singing Lesson, The Stranger, At The Bay

GLOSSARY:

Bohemian: Socially unconventional in an artistic way
Disillusion: The state of having been or the process of becoming free from false belief.
Genteel: Polished or characterized by exaggerated or affected politeness
Archangels: An angel of high rank
Marquee: A large tent used for social or commercial functions
Staves: Narrow strips of wood or narrow iron plates placed edge to edge to form the sides to create a structure
Baize: A coarse, typically green woollen material resembling felt, used for covering billiard and card tables
Sordid: Dirty or squalid

Virginia Woolf, England
(January 25, 1882 – March 28th, 1941)

The British writer, Virginia Woolf, is recognised as one of the most innovative writers of the twentieth century. Woolf's experimentation introduced an unconventional writing style, brought a new interpretation of time that added depth to the recurring thoughts in the conscious mind. She used stream of consciousness technique to create personality caverns behind her characters, which went on to impact the modernist movement of her period.

Born as Virginia Adeline Stephen, she was close to her family. When her mother, father and brother died in quick succession, she suffered from poor mental health and had a few mental breakdowns. While this sadness lasted for much of her life, she began to write to cope with her feelings.

Woolf along with the literary genius people of her times, went on to form the Bloomsbury group. She married Leonard Woolf and in 1917, found the Hogarth Press that published writers such as T S Eliot, Sigmund Freud, Katherine Mansfield, E M Forster, and also themselves.

Woolf wrote throughout her life. She produced novels, essays and short stories for children. Her novels, *Mrs Dalloway* (1925) and *To the Lighthouse* (1927), bring out the engaging technique of stream of consciousness as she seeks to portray the experience of thinking, in all of its chaos and distractions. Her work captures the fast-changing world in which she was working, from transformations in gender roles, sexuality and class to technologies such as cars, aeroplanes and cinema. Influenced by seminal writers and artists of the period such as Marcel Proust, Igor Stravinsky and the Post-Impressionists,* Woolf not only attempts to relay a character's thoughts, but also makes the reader experience those very thoughts in the same way as the character is thinking them.

Her volatile mental health worsened in 1941. Despite this tragic end, her works make her a frequent subject of study and inspire generations of women.

The Widow and The Parrot

Some fifty years ago Mrs Gage, an elderly widow, was sitting in her cottage in a village called Spilsby in Yorkshire. Although lame, and rather short sighted she was doing her best to mend a pair of clogs, for she had only a few shillings* a week to live on. As she hammered at the clog, the postman opened the door and threw a letter into her lap.

It bore the address 'Messrs Stagg and Beetle, 67 High Street, Lewes, Sussex.' Mrs Gage opened it and read:

'Dear Madam; We have the honor to inform you of the death of your brother Mr Joseph Brand.'

'Lawk a mussy.*' said Mrs Gage. 'Old brother Joseph gone at last!'

'He has left you his entire property,' the letter went on, 'which consists of a dwelling house, stable, cucumber frames, mangles, wheelbarrows, etc. etc., in the village of Rodmell, near Lewes. also bequeaths to you his entire fortune: Viz: £3.000. (three thousand pounds) sterling.'

Mrs Gage almost fell into the fire with joy. She had not seen her brother for many years, and, as he did not even acknowledge the Christmas card which she sent him every year, she thought that his miserly habits, well known to her from childhood, made him grudge even a penny stamp for a reply.

But now it had all turned out to her advantage. With three thousand pounds, to say nothing of house, etc., etc.. she and her family could live in great luxury for ever.

She determined that she must visit Rodmell at once. The village clergyman, the Rev Samuel Tallboys, lent her two pound ten, to pay her fare, and by next day all preparations for her journey were complete. The most important of these was the care of her dog Shag during her absence, for in spite of her poverty she was devoted to animals. and often went short herself rather than stint* her dog of his bone.

She reached Lewes late on Tuesday night. In those days, I must tell you, there was no bridge over the river at Southease, nor had the road to Newhaven yet been made. To reach Rodmell it was necessary to cross the river Ouse by a ford,* traces of which still exist, but this could only be attempted at low tide, when the stones on the riverbed appeared above the water. Mr Stacey, the farmer, was going to Rodmell in his cart, and he kindly offered to take Mrs Gage with him. They reached Rodmell about nine o'clock on a November night and Mr Stacey obligingly pointed out to Mrs Gage the house at the end of the village which had been left her by her brother. Mrs Gage knocked at the door. There was no answer. She knocked again. A very strange high voice shrieked out 'Not at home.' She was so much taken aback that if she had not heard footsteps coming she would have run away. However, the door was opened by an old village woman, by name Mrs Ford.

'Who was that shrieking out 'Not at home'?' said Mrs Gage.

'Drat the bird!' said Mrs Ford very peevishly,* pointing to a large gray parrot. 'He almost screams my head off. There he sits all day humped up on his perch like a monument screeching 'Not at home' if ever you go near his perch.' He was a very handsome bird, as Mrs Gage could see; but his feathers were sadly neglected. 'Perhaps he is unhappy, or he may be hungry,' she said. But Mrs Ford said it was temper merely; he was a seaman's parrot and had learnt his language in the east. However, she added, Mr Joseph was very fond of him, had called him James; and, it was said, talked to him as if he were a rational being. Mrs Ford soon left. Mrs Gage at once went to her box and fetched some sugar which she had with her and offered it to the parrot, saying in a very kind tone that she meant him no harm, but was his old master's sister, come to take possession of the house, and she would see to it that he was as happy as a bird could be. Taking a lantern she next went round the house to see what sort of property her brother had left her. It was a bitter disappointment. There were holes in all the carpets. The bottoms of the chairs had fallen out. Rats ran along the mantelpiece. There were large toadstools growing through the kitchen floor. There was not a stick of furniture worth seven pence halfpenny; and Mrs Gage only cheered herself by thinking of the three thousand pounds that lay safe and snug in Lewes Bank.

She determined to set off to Lewes next day in order to claim her money from Messrs Stagg and Beetle the solicitors. and then to return home as quick as she could. Mr Stacey, who was going in to market with some fine Berkshire pigs, again offered to take her with him, and told her some terrible stories of young people who had been drowned through trying to cross the river at high tide, as they drove. A great disappointment was in store for the poor old woman directly she got in to Mr Stagg's office.

'Pray take a seat, Madam,' he said, looking very solemn and grunting slightly. 'The fact is,' he went on, 'that you must prepare to face some very disagreeable news. Since I wrote to you I have gone carefully through Mr Brand's papers. I regret to say that I can find no trace whatever of the three thousand pounds. Mr Beetle, my partner, went himself to Rodmell and searched the premises with the utmost care. He found absolutely nothing—no gold, silver, or valuables of any kind—except a fine gray parrot which I advise you to sell for whatever he will fetch. His language. Benjamin Beetle said, is very extreme. But that is neither here nor there. I much fear you have had your journey for nothing. The premises are dilapidated;* and of course our expenses are considerable.' Here he stopped, and Mrs Gage well knew that he wished her to go. She was almost crazy with disappointment. Not only had she borrowed two pound ten from the Rev. Samuel Tallboys, but she would return home absolutely empty handed, for the parrot James would have to be sold to pay her fare. It was raining hard, but Mr Stagg did not press her to stay, and she was too beside herself with sorrow to care what she did. In spite of the rain she started to walk back to Rodmell across the meadows.

Mrs Gage as I have already said, was lame in her right leg. At the best of times she walked slowly, and now, what with her disappointment and the mud on the bank, her progress was very slow indeed. As she plodded* along, the day grew darker and darker until it was as much as she could do to keep on the raised path by the river side. You might have heard her grumbling as she walked, and complaining of her crafty brother Joseph, who had put her to all this trouble 'Express,' she said. 'to plague me. He was always a cruel little boy when we were children,' she went on. 'He liked worrying the poor insects, and I've known him trim a hairy caterpillar with a pair of scissors before my very eyes. He was such a miserly varmint* too. He used to hide his pocket money in a tree, and if anyone gave him a piece of iced cake for tea, he cut the sugar off and kept it for his supper. I make no doubt he's all aflame at this very moment in fire, but what's the comfort of that to me?' she asked, and indeed it was very little comfort, for she ran slap into a great cow which was coming along the bank, and rolled over and over in the mud.

She picked herself up as best she could and trudged* on again. It seemed to her that she had been walking for hours. It was now pitch dark and she could scarcely see her own hand before her nose. Suddenly she bethought her of Farmer Stacey's words about the ford. 'Lawk a mussy,' she said, 'however shall I find my way across? If the tide's in, I shall step into deep water and be swept out to sea in a jiffy!* Many's the couple that been drowned here: to say nothing of horses, carts, herds of cattle, and stacks of hay.'

Indeed what with the dark and the mud she had got herself into a pretty pickle. She could hardly see the river itself, let alone tell whether she had reached the ford or not. No lights were visible anywhere, for, as you may be aware, there is no cottage or house on that side of the river nearer than Asheham House, lately the seat of Mr Leonard Woolf. It seemed that there was nothing for it but to sit down and wait for the morning. But at her age, with the rheumatics* in her system, she might well die of cold. On the other hand, if she tried to cross the river it was almost certain that she would be drowned. So miserable was her state that she would gladly have changed places with one of the cows in the field. No more wretched old woman could have been found in the whole county of Sussex; standing on the river bank, not knowing whether to sit or to swim, or merely to roll over in the grass, wet though it was, and sleep or freeze to death, as her fate decided.

At that moment a wonderful thing happened. An enormous light shot up into the sky, like a gigantic torch lighting up every blade of grass. and showing her the ford not twenty yards away. It was low tide, and the crossing would be an easy matter if only the light did not go out before she had got over.

'It must be a comet or some such wonderful monstrosity,' she said as she hobbled* across. She could see the village of Rodmell brilliantly lit up in front of her.

'Bless us and save us!' she cried out. 'There's a house on fire—thanks be to the Lord'—for she reckoned that it would take some minutes at least to burn a house down, and in that time she would be well on her way to the village.

'It's an ill wind that blows nobody any good,' she said as she hobbled along the Roman road. Sure enough, she could see every inch of the way, and was almost in the village street when for the first time it struck her: 'Perhaps it's my own house that's blazing to cinders* before my very eyes!'

She was perfectly right. A small boy in his nightgown came capering up to her and cried out. 'Come and see old Joseph Brand's house ablaze!'

All the villagers were standing in a ring round the house handing buckets of water which were filled from the well in Monk's house kitchen. and throwing them on the flames. But the fire had got a strong hold. and just as Mrs Gage arrived, the roof fell.

'Has anybody saved the parrot?' she cried.

'Be thankful you're not inside yourself, Madam,' said the Rev. James Hawkesford, the clergyman. 'Do not worry for the dumb creatures. I make no doubt the parrot was mercifully suffocated on his perch.'

But Mrs Gage was determined to see for herself. She had to be held back by the village people, who remarked that she must be crazy to hazard her life for a bird.

'Poor old woman.' said Mrs Ford, 'she has lost all her property, save one old wooden box, with her night things in it. No doubt we should be crazed in her place too.'

So saying, Mrs Ford took Mrs Gage by the hand and led her off to her own cottage, where she was to sleep the night. The fire was now extinguished, and everybody went home to bed. But poor Mrs Gage could not sleep. She tossed and tumbled thinking of her miserable state, and wondering how she could get back to Yorkshire and pay the Rev. Samuel Tallboys the money she owed him. At the same time she was even more grieved to think of the fate of the poor parrot James. She had taken a liking to the bird, and thought that he must have an affectionate heart to mourn so deeply for the death of old Joseph Brand, who had never done a kindness to any human creature. It was a terrible death for an innocent bird, she thought: and if only she had been in time, she would have risked her own life to save his.

She was lying in bed thinking these thoughts when a slight tap at the window made her start. The tap was repeated three times over. Mrs Gage got out of bed as quickly as she could and went to the window. There, to her utmost surprise, sitting on the window ledge, was an enormous parrot. The rain had stopped and it was a fine moonlight night. She was greatly alarmed at first, but soon recognized the gray parrot, James, and was overcome with joy at his escape. She opened the window, stroked his head several times, and told him to come in. The parrot replied by gently shaking his head from side to side, then flew to the ground, walked away a few steps, looked back as if to see whether Mrs Gage were coming, and then returned to the window sill, where she stood in amazement.

'The creature has more meaning in its acts than we humans know,' she said to herself. 'Very well, James.' she said aloud, talking to him as though he were a human being, 'I'll take your word for it. Only wait a moment while I make myself decent.'

So saying she pinned on a large apron, crept as lightly as possible downstairs, and let herself out without rousing Mrs Ford. The parrot James was evidently satisfied. He now hopped briskly a few yards ahead of her in the direction of the burnt house. Mrs Gage followed as fast as she could. The parrot hopped, as if he knew his way perfectly, round to the back of the house, where the kitchen had originally been. Nothing now remained of it except the brick floor, which was still dripping with the water which had been thrown to put out the fire. Mrs Gage stood still in amazement while James hopped about, pecking here and there, as if he were testing the bricks with his beak. It was a very uncanny sight. and had not Mrs Gage been in the habit of living with animals, she would have lost her head, very likely, and hobbled back home. But stranger things yet were to happen. All this time the parrot had not said a word. He suddenly got into a state of the greatest excitement, fluttering his wings, tapping the floor repeatedly with his beak, and crying so shrilly. 'Not at home! Not at home!' that Mrs Gage feared that the whole village would be roused.

'Don't take on so, James: you'll hurt yourself,' she said soothingly. But he repeated his attack on the bricks more violently than ever.

'Whatever can be the meaning of it?' said Mrs Gage, looking carefully at the kitchen floor. The moonlight was bright enough to show her a slight unevenness in the laying of the bricks, as if they had been taken up and then relaid not quite flat with the others. She had fastened her apron with a large safety pin, and she now prized this pin between the bricks and found that they were only loosely laid together. Very soon she had taken one up in her hands. No sooner had she done this than the parrot hopped onto the brick next to it, and, tapping it smartly with his beak, cried, 'Not at home!' which Mrs Gage understood to mean that she was to move it. So they went on taking up the bricks in the moonlight until they had laid bare a space some six feet by four and a half. This the parrot seemed to think was enough. But what was to be done next?

Mrs Gage now rested, and determined to be guided entirely by the behavior of the parrot James. She was not allowed to rest for long. After scratching about in the sandy foundations for a few minutes, as you may have seen a hen scratch in the sand with her claws, he unearthed what at first looked like a round lump of yellowish stone. His excitement became so intense that Mrs Gage now went to his help. To her amazement she found that the whole space which they had uncovered was packed with long rolls of these round yellow stones, so neatly laid together that it was quite a job to move them. But what could they be? And for what purpose had they been hidden here? It was not until they had removed the entire layer on the top, and next a piece of oilcloth which lay beneath them, that a most miraculous sight was displayed before their eyes—there, in row after row, beautifully polished, and shining brightly in the moon light, were thousands of brand new sovereigns!*

This, then, was the miser's hiding place; and he had made sure that no one would detect it by taking two extraordinary precautions. In the first place, as was proved later, he had built a kitchen range over the spot where his treasure lay hid. so that unless the fire had destroyed it, no one could have guessed its existence; and secondly he had coated the top layer of sovereigns with some sticky substance, then rolled them in the earth, so that if by any chance one had been laid bare no one would have suspected that it was anything but a pebble such as you may see for yourself any day in the garden. Thus, it was only by the extraordinary coincidence of the fire and the parrot's sagacity* that old Joseph's craft was defeated.

Mrs Gage and the parrot now worked hard and removed the whole hoard—which numbered three thousand pieces, neither more nor less—placing them in her apron which was spread upon the ground. As the three thousandth coin was placed on the top of the pile, the parrot flew up into the air in triumph and alighted very gently on the top of Mrs Gage's head. It was in this fashion that they returned to Mrs Ford's cottage, at a very slow pace, for Mrs Gage was lame, as I have said, and now she was almost weighted to the ground by the contents of her apron. But she reached her room without anyone knowing of her visit to the ruined house.

Next day she returned to Yorkshire. Mr Stacey once more drove her into Lewes and was rather surprised to find how heavy Mrs Gage's wooden box had become. But he was a quiet sort of man, and merely concluded that the kind people at Rodmell had given her a few odds and ends to console her for the dreadful loss of all her property in the fire.

Out of sheer goodness of heart Mr Stacey offered to buy the parrot off her for half a crown; but Mrs Gage refused his offer with such indignation,* saying that she would not sell the bird for all the wealth of the Indies, that he concluded that the old woman had been crazed by her troubles.

It now only remains to be said that Mrs Gage got back to Spilsby in safety: took her black box to the Bank; and lived with James the parrot and her dog Shag in great comfort and happiness to a very great age.

It was not till she lay on her deathbed that she told the clergyman (the son of the Rev. Samuel Tallboys) the whole story, adding that she was quite sure that the house had been burnt on purpose by the parrot James, who, being aware of her danger on the river bank, flew into the scullery, and upset the oil stove which was keeping some scraps warm for her dinner. By this act, he not only saved her from drowning, but brought to light the three thousand pounds, which could have been found in no other manner. Such, she said is the reward of kindness to animals.

The clergyman thought that she was wandering in her mind. But it is certain that the very moment the breath was out of her body, James the parrot shrieked out, 'Not at home! Not at home!' and fell off his perch stone dead. The dog Shag had died some years previously.

Visitors to Rodmell may still see the ruins of the house, which was burnt down fifty years ago, and it is commonly said that if you visit it in the moonlight you may hear a parrot tapping with his beak upon the brick floor, while others have seen an old woman sitting there in a white apron.

If you liked reading this story, you must also read:

The Duchess and The Jeweller, The New Dress, The Mark on the Wall

---

GLOSSARY:

Post-Impressionists: A movement that emerged as a reaction against Impressionism (that sought to express their perceptions of nature, rather than create exact representations) and its concern for the naturalistic depiction of light and colour

Shillings: A former British coin and monetary unit equal to one-twentieth of a pound or twelve pence

Lawk a mussy: A corrupted version of 'Lord have mercy' presumably deliberately corrupted to avoid taking the name of the Lord in vain
Stint: Limiting supply
Ford: To cross a river or a stream at a shallow place
Peevishly: Having or showing an irritable disposition
Dilapidated: To be in a state of disrepair or ruin as a result of age or neglect
Plodded: To walk doggedly and slowly with heavy steps
Varmint: A troublesome wild animal.
Trudged: To walk slowly and with heavy steps, typically because of exhaustion or harsh conditions.
Jiffy: A very short time or moment
Rheumatics: Conditions characterized by inflammation or pain in muscles, joints, or fibrous tissue
Hobbled: To walk in an awkward way, typically because of pain from an injury
Cinders: A small piece of partly burnt coal or wood that has stopped giving off flames but still has a combustible matter in it
Sovereigns: A former British gold coin worth one pound sterling, now only minted for commemorative purposes
Sagacity: The quality of being sagacious or wise
Indignation: Resentment or anger

Carmen Dolores, Brazil

Pseudonym of Emília Moncorvo Bandeira de Melo
(March 11, 1852 – August 16, 1910)

Carmen Dolores, the pseudonym of the Brazilian writer, Emília Moncorvo Bandeira de Melo, was published under numerous pen names, although it was with this name that her identity became most well known throughout her creative career. She wrote novels, dramas, short tales, literary criticism, and countless journalistic essays in Portuguese that make her one of the most important female writers of Brazil.

Dolores was arguably most known for her chronicles, or brief reflections on Brazilian life, which appeared in her weekly column in *O Pas*. A collection of these works, *On the Fluttering of an Idea,* was released in 1910, reflecting her ongoing interest in women's rights. In her chronicles, she urged amending the law in Brazil to allow divorce and wrote strongly about equal rights, educational reform and the establishment of fair wage legislation.

Dolores also wrote *The Struggle,* which was published shortly after her death in 1911. Her work focuses on middle-class women in urban Brazil and her debut book, *Gradation* (1897), was a collection of short stories that addressed women's mostly dependent relationships with males.

Through her life and work, Dolores undertook the crusade of vindicating women's roles in Brazilian society, emphasizing women's rights to receive an education and to work. Her legacy testimonies her campaigns for basic freedoms and provide a deeper understanding of women's place in turn-of-the-century Brazil as well the country's literary traditions.

Aunt Zeze's Tears

Pale and thin, for eighteen years she had lived with her youngest sister, who had married very early and now possessed five children: two young ladies of marriageable age, a third still in short dresses, and two little boys.

Maria-José, whose nickname was Zézé, had never been beautiful or winning. Upon her father's death it was thought best that she should go to live with her sister Engracigna's family. Here she led a monotonous existence, helping to bring up her nephews and nieces, who were born in that young and happy household with a regularity that brooked small intervals between the births.

A long, pointed nose disfigured her face, and her lips, extremely thin, looked like a pale crack.

Her thoughtful gaze alone possessed a certain melancholy attractiveness. But even here, her eyes, protruding* too far for the harmony of the lines upon her face seemed always to be red, and her brows narrow and sparse.

Of late, an intricate network of wrinkles as fine as hairs, had formed at the corner of her eyes. From her nose, likewise, two furrows ran along the transparent delicacy of her skin and reached either side of her mouth. When she smiled, these wrinkles would cover her countenance with a mask of premature age, and threatened soon to disfigure her entirely. And yet, from habit, and through passive obedience to routine, Maria-José continued to dress like a young girl of eighteen, in brightly colored gowns, thin waists and white hats that ill became her frail and oldish face.

She would remain for a long time in painful indecision when it was a matter of picking out some piece of goods that was of too bright a red or blue,—as if instinctively she understood the disharmony of these hues with her age, whose rapid oncoming they moreover placed in all the more noticeable contrast. And at such times Engracigna and her daughters would say to her with a vehemence whose effect they little guessed, 'Why, Zézé! Buy something and be done with it! ... How silly! Do you want to dress like a widow? What a notion!'

And at bottom they meant it.

None of them saw Maria-José as she really was. Living with her day by day had served to efface the actual appearance of the faded old maid. For, in the minds of the mother and her daughters, who were moreover of a frivolous and indifferent sort, Zézé had grown to be the type, very vague, to be sure, but the eternal type of young girl of marriagable years who always should be well dressed and smiling.

When she would be out walking with her nieces, of sixteen and seventeen years, who wore the same clothes as she herself did, but whose graceful and lively charm became their gay colors of youth so well, Zézé's intelligence saw only too plainly the contrast between her and them; she would hold aloof from the laughing set, morose, wounded, as if oppressed by an unspeakable shame.

Ah! Who can depict the secret chagrin* of an old maid who sees pass by in useless monotony her dark, loveless, despairing days, without hope even of some event of personal interest, while about her moves the busy whirl of happier creatures whose life has but one goal, who feel emotions and tendernesses, and who look upon her simply as an obscure accessory in the household's affairs! They all loved her, of course, but not one of them suspected that she, too, could cherish those aspirations that are common to all human beings.

Her self-denial seemed to be a most natural

thing; indeed, they hardly considered her in the light of a living person; she was no longer of any consequence.

This was an attitude that satisfied the general egotism of the family, and to which they all had grown accustomed, never suspecting the grievous aspect of her sacrifice which was hidden by a sentiment of proud dignity.

So, when they would go to the theatre, and the box held only five—Engracigna, her husband, Fabio, and the three young ladies,—Maria-José knew beforehand that her sister, snugly wrapped in her opera-cloak, would come to her and say gently, in that purring voice of hers: 'You'll stay at home with the children tonight, won't you, Zézé? Little Paul isn't very well, and I wouldn't think of leaving him with anybody else. ...'

And she would remain behind, without betraying the revolt within her which, upon each occasion of these evidences of selfishness, would make the anemic blood in her veins tremble with agitation.

Alone in the dining-room she would ply her needle mechanically, while her nephews would amuse themselves with the toys scattered upon the table,—colored pictures and lead soldiers. Every other moment they would call her.

'Aunt Zézé, look at George pinching me!'

'I am not! Paul hit me first! ...'

And the good aunt would quiet them. Then, after both had been put to sleep in their little twin beds, she would rest her elbows upon the window-sill of her gloomy old-maid's room, and placing both hands beneath her sharp chin, her gaze directed towards heaven, she would lose herself in contemplation of the stars that shone in the limpid sky, less lonely, surely, than she upon earth. In vain did her eyes seek in the eyes of another that expression of sympathy and tenderness which alone would console her. ...

The truth is that Maria-José was suffering from the disappointment of unrequited passion. She had fallen in love with Monjardin, a poet and great friend of her brother-in-law, Fabio. Monjardin came to the house every Sunday.

Older than she, almost forty, but having preserved all the attractiveness of youth,—a black moustache, a vigorous, yet graceful figure, eyes still bright, charming and wide-awake,—Monjardin, without knowing it, had conquered Zézé.

This had come about in a rather curious manner. Finding the conversation of Fabio's wife and daughters too commonplace, Monjardin, when he would recite some of his poems or tell some story connected with his literary life, preferred to address Maria-José, whom he saw to be of a serious and impressive nature.

'Let's have another poem, please, Mr

Monjardin!' she would ask in supplicating tone. 'For instance, that one you call "Regrets." You know?'

And then he would describe in his verse the grief of a heart, disillusioned and broken by the cruelties of fate, that evoked in vain the remembrance of yesterday's lost loves, vanished in the mists of eternal despair.

He recited these bitter griefs in a strong, healthy man's voice, erect in the center of the parlor, looking mechanically, distractedly at Maria-José with his dreamy eyes; the concentrated effort of his memory brought to his face an involuntary immobility which Maria-José, most deliciously touched, drank in.

The poet had announced that he had written a poem which he would recite at Zézé's anniversary dinner. The date for this was but a few days distant, and ever since the poet's announcement the whole family had taken to teasing the old maid, christening her 'the muse of inspiration,' and asking her when the wedding would take place. ...

She smiled ingenuously; at such times her face would even take on an air of unusual happiness; her features grew animated, less wrinkled and more firm.

On the day of the celebration Maria-José came out of her room radiant with hope. At the belt of her white dress bloomed a rose; a little blood, set pulsing by her agitated heart, brought a feeble color to her marble cheeks, from which now protruded her long nose in a manner less displeasing than usual.

'See, mamma,' remarked one of the nieces, 'doesn't Zézé look like a young girl today?'

They dined amidst merry chatter. Seated directly across from Monjardin, Maria-José, hiding her glances behind the fruit-bowls that covered the table, looked at him furtively without surfeit. Her poor heart beat as if it would burst, waiting in agonized suspense for the poem in which the poet, without doubt, was to declare his intimate feelings for her. Monjardin had already pointed to his pocket as a token that he had the verses with him, and Zézé had trembled with gratification as she bashfully lowered her long face.

Champagne sparkled in the glasses and toasts were given. Several guests of distinction spoke first, then followed the hosts and their children,—frolicsome little things. Finally Monjardin arose and unfolded a manuscript, asking permission to declaim the verses which he had composed in honor of Maria-José, the central figure of the occasion. The guests greeted his remarks with noisy and enthusiastic approbation.*

'Hear! Hear!'

Engracigna and her daughters leaned over and cast malicious glances in the direction of Maria-José, but she was paying no attention to them. Her ears were buzzing; it seemed that everything was turning round.

Monjardin, the center of all eyes, made pompous preparation; he pulled down his vest, arranged his sleeves and, in sonorous, cadenced voice began to recite his alexandrines,* scanning the lines impeccably.

His poem opened with a eulogy of the ineffable* virtue, compounded of self-abnegation and chastity, that distinguished the angelic creature who, with her white tutelary* wings, watched over the happiness of his dear friend's love nest. He then recalled that the date of this day commemorated the happy birth of a being of immaculate purity, Maria-José, a veritable* saint who had renounced all her own aspirations so that she might consecrate* herself entirely to the duties of her sister's family; gentle figure of the mother-guardian, who would soon be the beloved grandmother sharing with her sister the joys of younger households which would soon be formed, offsprings of that home which her devoted tenderness as aunt and sister at present cultivated. As he came to a close, the poet raised his cup of sparkling wine and, in exalted voice, drank to the health of Zézé amidst the loud huzzahs of all present.

'Long live Aunt Zézé! Hurrah for Aunt Zézé!' cried the children, glass in hand, while the nieces laughed loudly, blushing to the ears, for they had understood very well the poet's reference to future 'younger households.'

Fabio and his wife, their eyes somewhat brightened by the strong champagne, proposed in turn their toast to Zézé.

'Here's to Zézé and the eighteen happy years we've lived together! ...'

Maria-José, as soon as she had seized the significance of Monjardin's verses, had grown deathly pale; stricken by sudden disillusionment, she felt a glacial chill overwhelm her body to the very marrow; she feared that she would faint straightway and provide a spectacle for the guests, who were all drinking her health, their eyes focussed upon her. A veil of tears spread before her sight.... In vain she tried to repress them, to force a smile of thanks upon her face. The smile wrinkled into a dolorous* grimace; she succeeded only in convulsing her contracted visage* with the sobs that she sought to restrain. Overcome at last, humiliated, powerless, she broke into tears, and this unforeseen denouement put an end at once to all the pleasure of the dinner.

'Zézé! Zézé! What ails you? ...'

Engracigna had rushed to her side in alarm; everyone rose, seeking the reason for the outburst; they surrounded the poor creature, whose head had sunk upon the table, in the midst of the rose petals, the fruits and the glasses which were strewn in charming confusion.

'What is the trouble? ...'

A nervous attack, perhaps? ... Confusion produced in her by the touching poem? ...

Finally they raised Maria-José's head and bathed it in cool water; whereupon the face of the poor old maid stood revealed in all the ugliness that her spasms of convulsive weeping cast over it, with her large aquiline* nose, her protruding eyes and her livid lips ...

And now Monjardin drew near. Delicately raising the icy fingers of Maria-José he lifted them to the edge of his perfumed moustache and placed upon them a grateful kiss; then, turning to Engracigna's daughters he said, with a solemn, self-complacent tone, 'Aunt Zézé's tears are the most beautiful homage that could be rendered to my poor verses.'

If you liked reading this story, you must also read:

A Drama in the Rock, To Fight, Complex Souls

GLOSSARY:

Protruding: Sticking out or projecting
Chagrin: Annoyance or distress at having failed or been humiliated.
Approbation: Approval or praise
Alexandrines: A term used for several distinct types of verse line with related metrical structures, most of which are ultimately derived from the classical French alexandrine
Ineffable: Something that is too great or extreme to be expressed or described in words
Tutelary: Serving as a protector or guardian
Veritable: A term used for emphasis, often to qualify a metaphor.
Consecrate: To make or declare sacred
Dolorous: Feeling or expressing great sorrow or distress
Visage: A person's facial expression
Aquiline: Usually as a description of a nose as hooked or curved like an eagle's beak

Arthur Conan Doyle, Scotland

(May 22, 1859 – July 7, 1930)

The Scottish writer, Arthur Conan Doyle, is best known for his creation of the detective character, Sherlock Holmes. Sir Arthur Ignatius Conan Doyle studied to become a doctor. While a medical student, Doyle was deeply intrigued by the talents of his professor, Dr Joseph Bell, who would closely observe the minutest detail regarding a patient's condition. This expertise in diagnostic reasoning became the model for Doyle's Sherlock Holmes, who first appeared in *A Study in Scarlet* (1887). He practised until 1891 and later, was knighted for his medical work in the second South African War and his public defence of the war in 1902.

Collections of Holmes' stories began flourishing with *The Adventures of Sherlock Holmes* (1892). Doyle experimented with fascination towards paranormal and spiritualism that led to stories like *The Mystery of Cloomber* (1888) and *The Coming of the Fairies* (1922). Doyle passed away in Windlesham, his home in Sussex. His last words were—'You are wonderful'—as addressed to his wife.

Doyle's legacy lives on through the legendary reworking of his infamous Sherlock Holmes across entertainment and literary circles. Sherlock Holmes has evolved beyond simply being an incredible character to becoming a cultural phenomenon that extends beyond the identity of the world's first and only 'consulting detective' who tracked criminals across continental Europe.

Today, Holmes is featured in countless books, series and movies, most of which weren't even written by his creator. The character has also been adapted into a BBC Series *Sherlock* that streams on Netflix.

Scandal in Bohemia

To Sherlock Holmes she is always the woman. I have seldom heard him mention her under any other name. In his eyes she eclipses and predominates the whole of her sex. It was not that he felt any emotion akin to love for Irene Adler. All emotions, and that one particularly, were abhorrent* to his cold, precise but admirably balanced mind. He was, I take it, the most perfect reasoning and observing machine that the world has seen, but as a lover he would have placed himself in a false position. He never spoke of the softer passions, save with a gibe* and a sneer.* They were admirable things for the observer—excellent for drawing the veil from men's motives and actions. But for the trained reasoner to admit such intrusions into his own delicate and finely adjusted temperament was to introduce a distracting factor which might throw a doubt upon all his mental results. Grit* in a sensitive instrument, or a crack in one of his own high-power lenses, would not be more disturbing than a strong emotion in a nature such as his. And yet there was but one woman to him, and that woman was the late Irene Adler, of dubious and questionable memory.

I had seen little of Holmes lately. My marriage had drifted us away from each other. My own complete happiness, and the home-centred interests which rise up around the man who first finds himself master of his own establishment, were sufficient to absorb all my attention, while Holmes, who loathed every form of society with his whole Bohemian soul, remained in our lodgings in Baker Street, buried among his old books, and alternating from week to week between cocaine and ambition, the drowsiness of the drug, and the fierce energy of his own keen nature. He was still, as ever, deeply attracted by the study of crime, and occupied his immense faculties and extraordinary powers of observation in following out those clues, and clearing up those mysteries which had been abandoned as hopeless by the official police. From time to time I heard some vague account of his doings: of his summons to Odessa in the case of the Trepoff murder, of his clearing up of the singular tragedy of the Atkinson brothers at Trincomalee, and finally of the mission which he had accomplished so delicately and successfully for the reigning family of Holland. Beyond these signs of his activity, however, which I merely shared with all the readers of the daily press, I knew little of my former friend and companion.

One night—it was on the twentieth of March, 1888—I was returning from a journey to a patient (for I had now returned to civil practice), when my way led me through Baker Street. As I passed the well-remembered door, which must always be associated in my mind with my wooing, and with the dark incidents of the Study in Scarlet, I was seized with a keen desire to see Holmes again, and to know how he was employing his extraordinary powers. His rooms were brilliantly lit, and, even as I looked up, I saw his tall, spare figure pass twice in a dark silhouette* against the blind. He was pacing the room swiftly, eagerly, with his head sunk upon his chest and his hands clasped behind him. To me, who knew his every mood and habit, his attitude and manner told their own story. He was at work again. He had risen out of his drug-created dreams and was hot upon the scent of some new problem. I rang the bell and was shown up to the chamber which had formerly been in part my own.

His manner was not effusive. It seldom was; but he was glad, I think, to see me. With hardly a word spoken, but with a kindly eye, he waved me to an armchair, threw across his case of cigars, and indicated a spirit case and a gasogene* in the corner. Then he stood before the fire and looked me over in his singular introspective fashion.

'Wedlock suits you,' he remarked. 'I think, Watson that you have put on seven and a half pounds since I saw you.'

'Seven!' I answered.

'Indeed, I should have thought a little more. Just a trifle more, I fancy, Watson. And in practice again, I observe. You did not tell me that you intended to go into harness.'

'Then, how do you know?'

'I see it, I deduce it. How do I know that you have been getting yourself very wet lately, and that you have a most clumsy and careless servant girl?'

'My dear Holmes,' said I, 'this is too much. You would certainly have been burned, had you lived a few centuries ago. It is true that I had a country walk on Thursday and came home in a dreadful mess, but as I have changed my clothes I can't imagine how you deduce it. As to Mary Jane, she is incorrigible,* and my wife has given her notice, but there, again, I fail to see how you work it out.'

He chuckled to himself and rubbed his long, nervous hands together.

'It is simplicity itself,' said he; 'My eyes tell me that on the inside of your left shoe, just where the firelight strikes it, the leather is scored by six almost parallel cuts. Obviously they have been caused by someone who has very carelessly scraped round the edges of the sole in order to remove crusted mud from it. Hence, you see, my double deduction that you had been out in vile* weather, and that you had a particularly malignant* boot-slitting specimen of the London slavey. As to your practice, if a gentleman walks into my rooms smelling of iodoform,* with a black mark of nitrate of silver upon his right forefinger, and a bulge on the right side of his top-hat to show where he has secreted his stethoscope, I must be dull, indeed, if I do not pronounce him to be an active member of the medical profession.'

I could not help laughing at the ease with which he explained his process of deduction. 'When I hear you give your reasons,' I remarked, 'the thing always appears to me to be so ridiculously simple that I could easily do it myself, though at each successive instance of your reasoning I am baffled* until you explain your process. And yet I believe that my eyes are as good as yours.'

'Quite so,' he answered, lighting a cigarette, and throwing himself down into an armchair. 'You see, but you do not observe. The distinction is clear. For example, you have frequently seen the steps which lead up from the hall to this room.'

'Frequently.'

'How often?'

'Well, some hundreds of times.'

'Then how many are there?'

'How many? I don't know.'

'Quite so! You have not observed. And yet, you have seen. That is just my point. Now, I know that there are seventeen steps, because I have both seen and observed. By the way, since you are interested in these little problems, and since you are good enough to chronicle one or two of my trifling experiences, you may be interested in this.' He threw over a sheet of thick, pink-tinted notepaper which had been lying open upon the table. 'It came by the last post,' said he. 'Read it aloud.'

The note was undated, and without either signature or address.

'There will call upon you to-night, at a quarter to eight o'clock,' it said, 'a gentleman who desires to consult you upon a matter of the very deepest moment. Your recent services to one of the royal houses of Europe have shown that you are one who may safely be trusted with matters which are of an importance which can hardly be exaggerated. This account of you we have from all quarters received. Be in your chamber then at that hour, and do not take it amiss if your visitor wear a mask.'

'This is indeed a mystery,' I remarked. 'What do you imagine that it means?'

'I have no data yet. It is a capital mistake to

theorise before one has data. Insensibly one begins to twist facts to suit theories, instead of theories to suit facts. But the note itself. What do you deduce from it?'

I carefully examined the writing, and the paper upon which it was written.

'The man who wrote it was presumably well to do,' I remarked, endeavouring to imitate my companion's processes. 'Such paper could not be bought under half a crown a packet. It is peculiarly strong and stiff.'

'Peculiar—that is the very word,' said Holmes. 'It is not an English paper at all. Hold it up to the light.'

I did so and saw a large 'E' with a small 'g,' a 'P,' and a large 'G' with a small 't' woven into the texture of the paper.

'What do you make of that?' asked Holmes.

'The name of the maker, no doubt; or his monogram, rather.'

'Not at all. The "G" with the small "t" stands for "Gesellschaft," which is the German for "Company." It is a customary contraction like our "Co." "P," of course, stands for "Papier." Now for the "Eg." Let us glance at our Continental Gazetteer.' He took down a heavy brown volume from his shelves. 'Eglow, Eglonitz—here we are, Egria. It is in a German-speaking country—in Bohemia, not far from Carlsbad. "Remarkable as being the scene of the death of Wallenstein, and for its numerous glass-factories and paper-mills." Ha, ha, my boy, what do you make of that?' His eyes sparkled, and he sent up a great blue triumphant cloud from his cigarette.

'The paper was made in Bohemia,' I said.

'Precisely. And the man who wrote the note is a German. Do you note the peculiar construction of the sentence—"This account of you we have from all quarters received." A Frenchman or Russian could not have written that. It is the German who is so uncourteous to his verbs. It only remains, therefore, to discover what is wanted by this German who writes upon Bohemian paper and prefers wearing a mask to showing his face. And here he comes, if I am not mistaken, to resolve all our doubts.'

As he spoke there was the sharp sound of horses' hoofs and grating wheels against the curb, followed by a sharp pull at the bell. Holmes whistled.

'A pair, by the sound,' said he. 'Yes,' he continued, glancing out of the window. 'A nice little brougham* and a pair of beauties. A hundred and fifty guineas apiece. There's money in this case, Watson, if there is nothing else.'

'I think that I had better go, Holmes.'

'Not a bit, Doctor. Stay where you are. I am lost without my Boswell. And this promises to be interesting. It would be a pity to miss it.'

'But your client—'

'Never mind him. I may want your help, and so may he. Here he comes. Sit down in that armchair, Doctor, and give us your best attention.'

A slow and heavy step, which had been heard upon the stairs and in the passage, paused immediately outside the door. Then there was a loud and authoritative tap.

'Come in!' said Holmes.

A man entered who could hardly have been less than six feet six inches in height, with the chest and limbs of a Hercules. His dress was rich with a richness which would, in England, be looked upon as akin to bad taste. Heavy bands of astrakhan* were slashed across the sleeves and fronts of his double-breasted coat, while the deep blue cloak which was thrown over his shoulders was lined with flame-coloured silk and secured at the neck with a brooch which consisted of a single flaming beryl.* Boots which extended halfway up his calves, and which were trimmed at the tops with rich brown fur, completed the impression of barbaric opulence* which was suggested by his whole appearance. He carried a broad-brimmed hat in his hand, while he wore across the upper part of his face, extending down past the cheekbones, a black vizard* mask, which he had apparently adjusted that very moment, for his hand was still raised to it as he entered. From the lower part of the face he appeared to be a man of strong character, with a thick, hanging lip, and a long, straight chin suggestive of resolution pushed to the length of obstinacy.*

'You had my note?' he asked with a deep harsh voice and a strongly marked German accent. 'I told you that I would call.' He looked from one to the other of us, as if uncertain which to address.

'Pray take a seat,' said Holmes. 'This is my friend and colleague, Dr Watson, who is occasionally good enough to help me in my cases. Whom have I the honour to address?'

'You may address me as the Count Von Kramm, a Bohemian nobleman. I understand that this gentleman, your friend, is a man of honour and discretion, whom I may trust with a matter of the most extreme importance. If not, I should much prefer to communicate with you alone.'

I rose to go, but Holmes caught me by the wrist and pushed me back into my chair. 'It is both, or none,' said he. 'You may say before this gentleman anything which you may say to me.'

The Count shrugged his broad shoulders. 'Then I must begin,' said he, 'by binding you both to absolute secrecy for two years; at the end of that time, the matter will be of no importance. At present it is not too much to say that it is of such weight it may have an influence upon European history.'

'I promise,' said Holmes.

'And I.'

'You will excuse this mask,' continued our strange visitor. 'The august person who employs me wishes his agent to be unknown to you, and I may confess at once that the title by which I have just called myself is not exactly my own.'

'I was aware of it,' said Holmes dryly.

'The circumstances are of great delicacy, and every precaution has to be taken to quench what might grow to be an immense scandal and seriously compromise one of the reigning families of Europe. To speak plainly, the matter implicates the great House of Ormstein, hereditary kings of Bohemia.'

'I was also aware of that,' murmured Holmes, settling himself down in his armchair and closing his eyes.

Our visitor glanced with some apparent surprise at the languid,* lounging figure of the man who had been no doubt depicted to him as the most incisive reasoner and most energetic agent in Europe. Holmes slowly reopened his eyes and looked impatiently at his gigantic client.

'If your Majesty would condescend to state your case,' he remarked, 'I should be better able to advise you.'

The man sprang from his chair and paced up and down the room in uncontrollable agitation. Then, with a gesture of desperation, he tore the mask from his face and hurled it upon the ground. 'You are right,' he cried; 'I am the King. Why should I attempt to conceal it?'

'Why, indeed?' murmured Holmes. 'Your Majesty had not spoken before I was aware that I was addressing Wilhelm Gottsreich Sigismond von Ormstein, Grand Duke of Cassel-Felstein, and hereditary King of Bohemia.'

'But you can understand,' said our strange visitor, sitting down once more and passing his hand over his high white forehead, 'you can understand that I am not accustomed to doing such business in my own person. Yet the matter was so delicate that I could not confide it to an agent without putting myself in his power. I have come incognito from Prague for the purpose of consulting you.'

'Then, pray consult,' said Holmes, shutting his eyes once more.

'The facts are briefly these: Some five years ago, during a lengthy visit to Warsaw, I made the acquaintance of the well-known adventuress, Irene Adler. The name is no doubt familiar to you.'

'Kindly look her up in my index, Doctor,' murmured Holmes without opening his eyes. For many years he had adopted a system of docketing all paragraphs concerning men and things, so that it was difficult to name a subject or a person on which he could not at once furnish information. In this case I found her biography sandwiched in between that of a Hebrew rabbi* and that of a staff-commander who had written a monograph upon the deep-sea fishes.

'Let me see!' said Holmes. 'Hum! Born in New Jersey in the year 1858. Contralto—hum! La Scala, hum! Prima donna Imperial Opera of Warsaw—yes! Retired from operatic stage—ha! Living in London—quite so! Your Majesty, as I understand, became entangled with this young person, wrote her some compromising letters, and is now desirous of getting those letters back.'

'Precisely so. But how—'

'Was there a secret marriage?'

'None.'

'No legal papers or certificates?'

'None.'

'Then I fail to follow your Majesty. If this young person should produce her letters for blackmailing or other purposes, how is she to prove their authenticity?'

'There is the writing.'

'Pooh, pooh! Forgery.'

'My private note-paper.'

'Stolen.'

'My own seal.'

'Imitated.'

'My photograph.'

'Bought.'

'We were both in the photograph.'

'Oh, dear! That is very bad! Your Majesty has indeed committed an indiscretion.*'

'I was mad—insane.'

'You have compromised yourself seriously.'

'I was only Crown Prince then. I was young. I am but thirty now.'

'It must be recovered.'

'We have tried and failed.'

'Your Majesty must pay. It must be bought.'

'She will not sell.'

'Stolen, then.'

'Five attempts have been made. Twice burglars in my pay ransacked her house. Once we diverted her luggage when she travelled. Twice she has been waylaid. There has been no result.'

'No sign of it?'

'Absolutely none.'

Holmes laughed. 'It is quite a pretty little problem,' said he.

'But a very serious one to me,' returned the King reproachfully.

'Very, indeed. And what does she propose to do with the photograph?'

'To ruin me.'

'But how?'

'I am about to be married.'

'So I have heard.'

'To Clotilde Lothman von Saxe-Meningen, second daughter of the King of Scandinavia. You may know the strict principles of her family. She is herself the very soul of delicacy. A shadow of a doubt as to my conduct would bring the matter to an end.'

'And Irene Adler?'

'Threatens to send them the photograph. And she will do it. I know that she will do it. You do not know her, but she has a soul of steel. She has the face of the most beautiful of women, and the mind of the most resolute* of men. Rather than I should marry another woman, there are no lengths to which she would not go-—none.'

'You are sure that she has not sent it yet?'

'I am sure.'

'And why?'

'Because she has said that she would send it on the day when the betrothal* was publicly proclaimed. That will be next Monday.'

'Oh, then we have three days yet,' said Holmes with a yawn. 'That is very fortunate, as I have one or two matters of importance to look into just at present. Your Majesty will, of course, stay in London for the present?'

'Certainly. You will find me at the Langham under the name of the Count Von Kramm.'

'Then I shall drop you a line to let you know how we progress.'

'Pray do so. I shall be all anxiety.'

'Then, as to money?'

'You have *carte blanche*.*'

'Absolutely?'

'I tell you that I would give one of the provinces of my kingdom to have that photograph.'

'And for present expenses?'

The King took a heavy chamois* leather bag from under his cloak and laid it on the table.

'There are three hundred pounds in gold and seven hundred in notes,' he said.

Holmes scribbled a receipt upon a sheet of his note-book and handed it to him.

'And Mademoiselle's address?' he asked.

'Is Briony Lodge, Serpentine Avenue, St. John's Wood.'

Holmes took a note of it. 'One other question,' said he. 'Was the photograph a cabinet?'

'It was.'

'Then, good-night, your Majesty, and I trust that we shall soon have some good news for you. And good-night, Watson,' he added, as the wheels of the royal brougham rolled down the street. 'If you will be good enough to call to-morrow afternoon at three o'clock I should like to chat this little matter over with you.'

II

At three o'clock precisely I was at Baker Street, but Holmes had not yet returned. The landlady informed me that he had left the house shortly after eight o'clock in the morning. I sat down beside the fire, however, with the intention of awaiting him, however long he might be. I was already deeply interested in his inquiry, for, though it was surrounded by none of the grim and strange features which were associated with the two crimes which I have already recorded, still, the nature of the case and the exalted station of his client gave it a character of its own. Indeed, apart from the nature of the investigation which my friend had on hand, there was something in his masterly grasp of a situation, and his keen, incisive reasoning, which made it a pleasure to me to study his system of work, and to follow the quick, subtle methods by which he disentangled the most inextricable* mysteries. So accustomed was I to his invariable success that the very possibility of his failing had ceased to enter into my head.

It was close upon four before the door opened, and a drunken-looking groom, ill-kempt* and side-whiskered, with an inflamed face and disreputable clothes, walked into the room. Accustomed as I was to my friend's amazing powers in the use of disguises, I had to look three times before I was certain that it was indeed he. With a nod he vanished into the bedroom, whence he emerged in five minutes tweed-suited and respectable, as of old. Putting his hands into his pockets, he stretched out his legs in front of the fire and laughed heartily for some minutes.

'Well, really!' he cried, and then he choked and laughed again until he was obliged to lie back, limp and helpless, in the chair.

'What is it?'

'It's quite too funny. I am sure you could never guess how I employed my morning, or what I ended by doing.'

'I can't imagine. I suppose that you have been watching the habits, and perhaps the house, of Miss Irene Adler.'

'Quite so; but the sequel was rather unusual. I will tell you, however. I left the house a little after eight o'clock this morning in the character of a groom out of work. There is a wonderful sympathy and freemasonry among horsey men. Be one of them, and you will know all that there is to know. I soon found Briony Lodge. It is a bijou* villa, with a garden at the back, but built out in front right up to the road, two stories. Chubb lock to the door. Large sitting-room on the right side, well furnished, with long windows almost to the floor, and those preposterous English window fasteners which a child could open. Behind there was nothing remarkable, save that the passage window could be reached from the top of the coach-house. I walked round it and examined it closely from every point of view, but without noting anything else of interest.

'I then lounged down the street and found, as I expected, that there was a mews* in a lane which runs down by one wall of the garden. I lent the ostlers* a hand in rubbing down their horses, and received in exchange twopence, a glass of half-and-half, two fills of shag tobacco, and as much information as I could desire about Miss Adler, to say nothing of half a dozen other people in the neighbourhood in whom I was not in the least interested, but whose biographies I was compelled to listen to.'

'And what of Irene Adler?' I asked.

'Oh, she has turned all the men's heads down in that part. She is the daintiest thing under a bonnet on this planet. So say the Serpentine-mews, to a man. She lives quietly, sings at concerts, drives out at five every day, and returns at seven sharp for dinner. Seldom goes out at other times, except when she sings. Has only one male visitor, but a good deal of him. He is dark, handsome, and dashing, never calls less than once a day, and often twice. He is a Mr Godfrey Norton, of the Inner Temple. See the advantages of a cabman as a confidant.* They had driven him home a dozen times from Serpentine-mews, and knew all about him. When I had listened to all they had to tell, I began to walk up and down near Briony Lodge once more and to think over my plan of campaign.

'This Godfrey Norton was evidently an

important factor in the matter. He was a lawyer. That sounded ominous. What was the relation between them, and what was the object of his repeated visits? Was she his client, his friend, or his mistress? If the former, she had probably transferred the photograph to his keeping. If the latter, it was less likely. On the issue of this question depended whether I should continue my work at Briony Lodge, or turn my attention to the gentleman's chambers in the Temple. It was a delicate point, and it widened the field of my inquiry. I fear that I bore you with these details, but I have to let you see my little difficulties, if you are to understand the situation.'

'I am following you closely,' I answered.

'I was still balancing the matter in my mind when a hansom cab drove up to Briony Lodge, and a gentleman sprang out. He was a remarkably handsome man, dark, aquiline, and moustached—evidently the man of whom I had heard. He appeared to be in a great hurry, shouted to the cabman to wait, and brushed past the maid who opened the door with the air of a man who was thoroughly at home.

'He was in the house about half an hour, and I could catch glimpses of him in the windows of the sitting-room, pacing up and down, talking excitedly, and waving his arms. Of her I could see nothing. Presently he emerged, looking even more flurried than before. As he stepped up to the cab, he pulled a gold watch from his pocket and looked at it earnestly, "Drive like the devil," he shouted, "first to Gross & Hankey's in Regent Street, and then to the Church of St. Monica in the Edgeware Road. Half a guinea if you do it in twenty minutes!"

'Away they went, and I was just wondering whether I should not do well to follow them when up the lane came a neat little landau,* the coachman with his coat only half-buttoned, and his tie under his ear, while all the tags of his harness were sticking out of the buckles. It hadn't pulled up before she shot out of the hall door and into it. I only caught a glimpse of her at the moment, but she was a lovely woman, with a face that a man might die for.

'"The Church of St. Monica, John," she cried, "and half a sovereign if you reach it in twenty minutes."

'This was quite too good to lose, Watson. I was just balancing whether I should run for it, or whether I should perch behind her landau when a cab came through the street. The driver looked twice at such a shabby fare, but I jumped in before he could object. "The Church of St. Monica," said I, "and half a sovereign if you reach it in twenty minutes." It was twenty-five minutes to twelve, and of course, it was clear enough what was in the wind.

'My cabby drove fast. I don't think I ever drove

faster, but the others were there before us. The cab and the landau with their steaming horses were in front of the door when I arrived. I paid the man and hurried into the church. There was not a soul there save the two whom I had followed and a surpliced* clergyman, who seemed to be expostulating* with them. They were all three standing in a knot in front of the altar. I lounged up the side aisle like any other idler who has dropped into a church. Suddenly, to my surprise, the three at the altar faced round to me, and Godfrey Norton came running as hard as he could towards me.

'"Thank god," he cried. "You'll do. Come! Come!"

'"What then?" I asked.

'"Come, man, come, only three minutes, or it won't be legal."

'I was half-dragged up to the altar, and before I knew where I was I found myself mumbling responses which were whispered in my ear, and vouching for things of which I knew nothing, and generally assisting in the secure tying up of Irene Adler, spinster, to Godfrey Norton, bachelor. It was all done in an instant, and there was the gentleman thanking me on the one side and the lady on the other, while the clergyman beamed on me in front. It was the most preposterous* position in which I ever found myself in my life, and it was the thought of it that started me laughing just now.

It seems that there had been some informality about their license, that the clergyman absolutely refused to marry them without a witness of some sort, and that my lucky appearance saved the bridegroom from having to sally out into the streets in search of a best man. The bride gave me a sovereign, and I mean to wear it on my watch-chain in memory of the occasion.'

'This is a very unexpected turn of affairs,' said I 'and what then?'

'Well, I found my plans very seriously menaced. It looked as if the pair might take an immediate departure, and so necessitate very prompt and energetic measures on my part. At the church door, however, they separated, he driving back to the Temple, and she to her own house. "I shall drive out in the park at five as usual," she said as she left him. I heard no more. They drove away in different directions, and I went off to make my own arrangements.'

'Which are?'

'Some cold beef and a glass of beer,' he answered, ringing the bell. 'I have been too busy to think of food, and I am likely to be busier still this evening. By the way, Doctor, I shall want your co-operation.'

'I shall be delighted.'

'You don't mind breaking the law?'

'Not in the least.'

'Nor running a chance of arrest?'

'Not in a good cause.'

'Oh, the cause is excellent!'

'Then I am your man.'

'I was sure that I might rely on you.'

'But what is it you wish?'

'When Mrs Turner has brought in the tray I will make it clear to you. Now,' he said as he turned hungrily on the simple fare that our landlady had provided, 'I must discuss it while I eat, for I have not much time. It is nearly five now. In two hours we must be on the scene of action. Miss Irene, or Madame, rather, returns from her drive at seven. We must be at Briony Lodge to meet her.'

'And what then?'

'You must leave that to me. I have already arranged what is to occur. There is only one point on which I must insist. You must not interfere, come what may. You understand?'

'I am to be neutral?'

'To do nothing whatever. There will probably be some small unpleasantness. Do not join in it. It will end in my being conveyed into the house. Four or five minutes afterwards the sitting-room window will open. You are to station yourself close to that open window.'

'Yes.'

'You are to watch me, for I will be visible to you.'

'Yes.'

'And when I raise my hand—so—you will throw into the room what I give you to throw, and will, at the same time, raise the cry of fire. You quite follow me?'

'Entirely.'

'It is nothing very formidable,' he said, taking a long cigar-shaped roll from his pocket. 'It is an ordinary plumber's smoke-rocket, fitted with a cap at either end to make it self-lighting. Your task is confined to that. When you raise your cry of fire, it will be taken up by quite a number of people. You may then walk to the end of the street, and I will rejoin you in ten minutes. I hope that I have made myself clear?'

'I am to remain neutral, to get near the window, to watch you, and at the signal to throw in this object, then to raise the cry of fire, and to wait you at the corner of the street.'

'Precisely.'

'Then you may entirely rely on me.'

'That is excellent. I think, perhaps, it is almost time that I prepare for the new role I have to play.'

He disappeared into his bedroom and returned in a few minutes in the character of an amiable and simple-minded Nonconformist* clergyman. His broad black hat, his baggy trousers, his white tie, his sympathetic smile, and general look of peering and benevolent* curiosity were such as Mr John

Hare alone could have equalled. It was not merely that Holmes changed his costume. His expression, his manner, his very soul seemed to vary with every fresh part that he assumed. The stage lost a fine actor, even as science lost an acute reasoner, when he became a specialist in crime.

It was a quarter past six when we left Baker Street, and it still wanted ten minutes to the hour when we found ourselves in Serpentine Avenue. It was already dusk, and the lamps were just being lighted as we paced up and down in front of Briony Lodge, waiting for the coming of its occupant. The house was just such as I had pictured it from Sherlock Holmes' succinct* description, but the locality appeared to be less private than I expected. On the contrary, for a small street in a quiet neighbourhood, it was remarkably animated. There was a group of shabbily dressed men smoking and laughing in a corner, a scissors-grinder with his wheel, two guardsmen who were flirting with a nurse-girl, and several well-dressed young men who were lounging up and down with cigars in their mouths.

'You see,' remarked Holmes, as we paced to and fro in front of the house, 'this marriage rather simplifies matters. The photograph becomes a double-edged weapon now. The chances are that she would be as averse to its being seen by Mr Godfrey Norton, as our client is to its coming to the eyes of his princess. Now the question is, where are we to find the photograph?'

'Where, indeed?'

'It is most unlikely that she carries it about with her. It is cabinet size. Too large for easy concealment about a woman's dress. She knows that the King is capable of having her waylaid and searched. Two attempts of the sort have already been made. We may take it, then, that she does not carry it about with her.'

'Where, then?'

'Her banker or her lawyer. There is that double possibility. But I am inclined to think neither. Women are naturally secretive, and they like to do their own secreting. Why should she hand it over to anyone else? She could trust her own guardianship, but she could not tell what indirect or political influence might be brought to bear upon a business man. Besides, remember that she had resolved to use it within a few days. It must be where she can lay her hands upon it. It must be in her own house.'

'But it has twice been burgled.'

'Pshaw! They did not know how to look.'

'But how will you look?'

'I will not look'

'What then?'

'I will get her to show me.'

'But she will refuse.'

'She will not be able to. But I hear the rumble

of wheels. It is her carriage. Now carry out my orders to the letter.'

As he spoke the gleam of the sidelights of a carriage came round the curve of the avenue. It was a smart little landau which rattled up to the door of Briony Lodge. As it pulled up, one of the loafing men at the corner dashed forward to open the door in the hope of earning a copper, but was elbowed away by another loafer, who had rushed up with the same intention. A fierce quarrel broke out, which was increased by the two guardsmen, who took sides with one of the loungers, and by the scissors-grinder, who was equally hot upon the other side. A blow was struck, and in an instant the lady, who had stepped from her carriage, was the centre of a little knot of flushed and struggling men, who struck savagely at each other with their fists and sticks. Holmes dashed into the crowd to protect the lady; but, just as he reached her, he gave a cry and dropped to the ground, with the blood running freely down his face. At his fall the guardsmen took to their heels in one direction and the loungers in the other, while a number of better dressed people, who had watched the scuffle without taking part in it, crowded in to help the lady and to attend to the injured man. Irene Adler, as I will still call her, had hurried up the steps; but she stood at the top with her superb figure outlined against the lights of the hall, looking back into the street.

'Is the poor gentleman much hurt?' she asked.

'He is dead,' cried several voices.

'No, no, there's life in him!' shouted another. 'But he'll be gone before you can get him to hospital.'

'He's a brave fellow,' said a woman. 'They would have had the lady's purse and watch if it hadn't been for him. They were a gang, and a rough one, too. Ah, he's breathing now.'

'He can't lie in the street. May we bring him in, marm?'

'Surely. Bring him into the sitting-room. There is a comfortable sofa. This way, please!'

Slowly and solemnly he was borne into Briony Lodge and laid out in the principal room, while I still observed the proceedings from my post by the window. The lamps had been lit, but the blinds had not been drawn, so that I could see Holmes as he lay upon the couch. I do not know whether he was seized with compunction* at that moment for the part he was playing, but I know that I never felt more heartily ashamed of myself in my life than when I saw the beautiful creature against whom I was conspiring, or the grace and kindliness with which she waited upon the injured man. And yet it would be the blackest treachery to Holmes to draw back now from the part which he had intrusted to me. I hardened my heart, and took the smoke-rocket from under my ulster. After all, I thought, we are not injuring her. We are but preventing her from injuring another.

Holmes had sat up upon the couch, and I saw him motion like a man who is in need of air. A maid rushed across and threw open the window. At the same instant I saw him raise his hand and at the signal I tossed my rocket into the room with a cry of 'Fire!' The word was no sooner out of my mouth than the whole crowd of spectators, well dressed and ill—gentlemen, ostlers, and servant maids—joined in a general shriek of 'Fire!' Thick clouds of smoke curled through the room and out at the open window. I caught a glimpse of rushing figures, and a moment later the voice of Holmes from within assuring them that it was a false alarm. Slipping through the shouting crowd I made my way to the corner of the street, and in ten minutes was rejoiced to find my friend's arm in mine, and to get away from the scene of uproar. He walked swiftly and in silence for some few minutes until we had turned down one of the quiet streets which lead towards the Edgeware Road.

'You did it very nicely, Doctor,' he remarked. 'Nothing could have been better. It is all right.'

'You have the photograph?'

'I know where it is.'

'And how did you find out?'

'She showed me, as I told you she would.'

'I am still in the dark.'

'I do not wish to make a mystery,' said he, laughing. 'The matter was perfectly simple. You, of course, saw that everyone in the street was an accomplice. They were all engaged for the evening.'

'I guessed as much.'

'Then, when the row broke out, I had a little moist red paint in the palm of my hand. I rushed forward, fell down, clapped my hand to my face, and became a piteous spectacle. It is an old trick.'

'That also I could fathom.'

'Then they carried me in. She was bound to have me in. What else could she do? And into her sitting-room, which was the very room which I suspected. It lay between that and her bedroom, and I was determined to see which. They laid me on a couch, I motioned for air, they were compelled to open the window, and you had your chance.'

'How did that help you?'

'It was all-important. When a woman thinks that her house is on fire, her instinct is at once to rush to the thing which she values most. It is a perfectly overpowering impulse, and I have more than once taken advantage of it. In the case of the Darlington Substitution Scandal, it was of use to me, and also in the Arnsworth Castle business. A married woman grabs at her baby; an unmarried one reaches for her jewel-box. Now it was clear to me that our lady of to-day had nothing in the house more precious to her than what we are in quest of. She would rush to secure it. The alarm of fire was admirably done. The smoke and shouting were enough to shake nerves of steel. She responded beautifully. The photograph is in a recess behind a sliding panel just above the right bell-pull. She was there in an instant, and I caught a glimpse of it as she half drew it out. When I cried out that it was a false alarm, she replaced it, glanced at the rocket, rushed from the room, and I have not seen her since. I rose, and, making my excuses, escaped from the house. I hesitated whether to attempt to secure the photograph at once; but the coachman had come in, and as he was watching me narrowly it seemed safer to wait. A little over-precipitance may ruin all.'

'And now?' I asked.

'Our quest is practically finished. I shall call with the King to-morrow, and with you, if you care to come with us. We will be shown into the sitting-room to wait for the lady, but it is probable that when she comes she may find neither us nor the photograph. It might be a satisfaction to his Majesty to regain it with his own hands.'

'And when will you call?'

'At eight in the morning. She will not be up, so that we shall have a clear field. Besides, we must be prompt, for this marriage may mean a complete change in her life and habits. I must wire to the King without delay.'

We had reached Baker Street and had stopped at the door. He was searching his pockets for the key when someone passing said:

'Good-night, Mister Sherlock Holmes.'

There were several people on the pavement at the time, but the greeting appeared to come from a slim youth in an ulster who had hurried by.

'I've heard that voice before,' said Holmes, staring down the dimly lit street. 'Now, I wonder who the deuce that could have been.'

III

I slept at Baker Street that night, and we were engaged upon our toast and coffee in the morning when the King of Bohemia rushed into the room.

'You have really got it!' he cried, grasping Sherlock Holmes by either shoulder and looking eagerly into his face.

'Not yet.'

'But you have hopes?'

'I have hopes.'

'Then, come. I am all impatience to be gone.'

'We must have a cab.'

'No, my brougham is waiting.'

'Then that will simplify matters.' We descended and started off once more for Briony Lodge.

'Irene Adler is married,' remarked Holmes.

'Married! When?'

'Yesterday.'

'But to whom?'

'To an English lawyer named Norton.'

'But she could not love him.'

'I am in hopes that she does.'

'And why in hopes?'

'Because it would spare your Majesty all fear of future annoyance. If the lady loves her husband, she does not love your Majesty. If she does not love your Majesty, there is no reason why she should interfere with your Majesty's plan.'

'It is true. And yet—! Well! I wish she had been of my own station! What a queen she would have made!' He relapsed into a moody silence, which was not broken until we drew up in Serpentine Avenue.

The door of Briony Lodge was open, and an elderly woman stood upon the steps. She watched us with a sardonic eye as we stepped from the brougham.

'Mr Sherlock Holmes, I believe?' said she.

'I am Mr Holmes,' answered my companion, looking at her with a questioning and rather startled gaze.

'Indeed! My mistress told me that you were likely to call. She left this morning with her husband by the 5:15 train from Charing Cross for the Continent.'

'What!' Sherlock Holmes staggered back, white

with chagrin and surprise. 'Do you mean that she has left England?'

'Never to return.'

'And the papers?' asked the King hoarsely. 'All is lost.'

'We shall see.' He pushed past the servant and rushed into the drawing-room, followed by the King and myself. The furniture was scattered about in every direction, with dismantled shelves and open drawers, as if the lady had hurriedly ransacked them before her flight. Holmes rushed at the bell-pull, tore back a small sliding shutter, and, plunging in his hand, pulled out a photograph and a letter. The photograph was of Irene Adler herself in evening dress, the letter was superscribed to 'Sherlock Holmes, Esq. To be left till called for.' My friend tore it open, and we all three read it together. It was dated at midnight of the preceding night and ran in this way:

'MY DEAR MR SHERLOCK HOLMES,—

You really did it very well. You took me in completely. Until after the alarm of fire, I had not a suspicion. But then, when I found how I had betrayed myself, I began to think. I had been warned against you months ago. I had been told that, if the King employed an agent, it would certainly be you. And your address had been given me. Yet, with all this, you made me reveal what you wanted to know. Even after

I became suspicious, I found it hard to think evil of such a dear, kind old clergyman. But, you know, I have been trained as an actress myself. Male costume is nothing new to me. I often take advantage of the freedom which it gives. I sent John, the coachman, to watch you, ran up stairs, got into my walking clothes, as I call them, and came down just as you departed.

'Well, I followed you to your door, and so made sure that I was really an object of interest to the celebrated Mr Sherlock Holmes. Then I, rather imprudently, wished you good-night, and started for the Temple to see my husband.

'We both thought the best resource was flight, when pursued by so formidable an antagonist; so you will find the nest empty when you call to-morrow. As to the photograph, your client may rest in peace. I love and am loved by a better man than he. The King may do what he will without hindrance from one whom he has cruelly wronged. I keep it only to safeguard myself, and to preserve a weapon which will always secure me from any steps which he might take in the future. I leave a photograph which he might care to possess; and I remain, dear Mr Sherlock Holmes,

'Very truly yours,

'IRENE NORTON, née ADLER.'

'What a woman—oh, what a woman!' cried the King of Bohemia, when we had all three read this epistle. 'Did I not tell you how quick and resolute she was? Would she not have made an admirable queen? Is it not a pity that she was not on my level?'

'From what I have seen of the lady, she seems, indeed to be on a very different level to your Majesty,' said Holmes coldly. 'I am sorry that I have not been able to bring your Majesty's business to a more successful conclusion.'

'On the contrary, my dear sir,' cried the King; 'nothing could be more successful. I know that her word is inviolate. The photograph is now as safe as if it were in the fire.'

'I am glad to hear your Majesty say so.'

'I am immensely indebted to you. Pray tell me in what way I can reward you. This ring—' He slipped an emerald snake ring from his finger and held it out upon the palm of his hand.

'Your Majesty has something which I should value even more highly,' said Holmes.

'You have but to name it.'

'This photograph!'

The King stared at him in amazement.

'Irene's photograph!' he cried. 'Certainly, if you wish it.'

'I thank your Majesty. Then there is no more to be done in the matter. I have the honour to wish you a very good-morning.' He bowed, and, turning away without observing the hand which the King had stretched out to him, he set off in my company for his chambers.

And that was how a great scandal threatened to affect the kingdom of Bohemia, and how the best plans of Mr Sherlock Holmes were beaten by a woman's wit. He used to make merry over the cleverness of women, but I have not heard him do it of late. And when he speaks of Irene Adler, or when he refers to her photograph, it is always under the honourable title of the woman.

If you liked reading this story, you must also read:

His Last Bow, A Study in Scarlet, The Hound of the Baskervilles

---

GLOSSARY:

Abhorrent: Inspiring disgust and loathing

Gibe: Taunt

Sneer: A contemptuous or mocking smile

Grit: Small loose particles of stone or sand

Silhouette: The dark shape and outline of someone or

something visible in restricted light against a brighter background.

Gasogene: A late Victorian device for producing carbonated water.

Incorrigible: Incurable, or a type of behaviour that cannot be changed or reformed.

Vile: Extremely unpleasant

Malignant: Evil in nature or effect

Iodoform: A yellow crystalline volatile compound CHI3 with a penetrating persistent odour that is used as an antiseptic dressing

Baffled: Perplexed or puzzled

Brougham: A horse-drawn carriage with a roof, four wheels, and an open driver's seat in front

Astrakhan: Closely-curled black and grey fleece of very young Karakul lambs from Astrakhan, Russia

Beryl: A silicate mineral found in jewellery and emeralds

Opulence: Great wealth or luxuriousness.

Vizard: A mask or disguise

Obstinacy: Stubbornness or inflexibility

Languid: Having or showing a disinclination for physical exertion or effort.

Rabbi: In Judaism, it refers to a person qualified by academic studies of the Hebrew Bible and the Talmud to act as spiritual leader and religious teacher of a Jewish community or congregation

Indiscretion: Displaying a lack of good knowledge

Resolute: Admirably purposeful, determined

Betrothal: Engagement to be married

Carte blanche: Complete freedom to act as one wishes
Chamois: A type of soft pliable leather now made from sheepskin or lambskin
Inextricable: Impossible to disentangle or separate
Ill-kempt: Untidy
Bijou: Something small and delicately worked, such as a trinket
Mews: A group of stables, typically with rooms above, built round a yard or along an alley
Ostlers: A man employed to look after the horses of people staying at an inn
Confidant: A person with whom one shares a secret or private matter, trusting them not to repeat it to others
Landau: A horse-drawn four-wheeled enclosed carriage with a removable front cover and a back cover that can be raised and lowered
Surplice: A loose white linen vestment varying from hip-length to calf-length, worn by clergy at Christian church services
Expostulating: Express strong disapproval or disagreement
Preposterous: Absurd or ridiculous
Nonconformist: A person who does not conform to an established church especially one who does not conform to the Church of England
Benevolent: Well-meaning and kindly.
Succinct: Brief and concise
Compunction: A feeling of guilt or moral scruple that prevents or follows the doing of something bad

Olive Schreiner, South Africa

(March 24, 1855 – December 11, 1920)

The South African writer, Olive Schreiner, had a powerful intellect. She was a radical feminist and held liberal views on politics and society. She was largely self-educated and very bright. She wished to be a doctor or a nurse, but lack of funds and her poor health stopped her from pursuing either of those professions.

She published *The Story of an African Farm* in 1883, which established her as a prominent novelist. Because there was a bias against female authors at that time, she authored the book under a pen name, Ralph Irons.[1]

Schreiner rejected her parents' Christian beliefs when she was fifteen years old, and rebelled against stereotypical images of women as dependent on men. She attacked British imperialism and racism in South Africa and championed the causes of the Boers and Black people. Schreiner also fought for equal pay and rights and spent her life as a troubled and mostly lonely person. She died at the age of sixty-five.

She believed in free-thinking, progressive views about marriage, premarital sex and pregnancy out of wedlock, and adds these as themes in *The Story of African Farm* where the main character, Lyndall, is an unconventional heroine who does not believe in God. It was revolutionary feminist writing of that time and the book became a best seller in Europe and the United States.

---

1 Many women writers would use pseudonyms as there was a general bias against them. Emily Bronte wrote under Ellis Bell, Mary Ann Evans wrote under George Eliot and even J. K. Rowling (the writer of the Harry Potter series!) is a pseudonym adopted by Joanne Rowling.

Dream Life and Real Life

A Little African Story

Little Jannita sat alone beside a milk-bush. Before her and behind her stretched the plain, covered with red sand and thorny karoo* bushes; and here and there a milk-bush, looking like a bundle of pale green rods tied together. Not a tree was to be seen anywhere, except on the banks of the river, and that was far away, and the sun beat on her head. Round her fed the Angora goats she was herding; pretty things, especially the little ones, with white silky curls that touched the ground. But Jannita sat crying. If an angel should gather up in his cup all the tears that have been shed, I think the bitterest would be those of children.

By and by she was so tired, and the sun was so hot, she laid her head against the milk-bush and dropped asleep.

She dreamed a beautiful dream. She thought that when she went back to the farmhouse in the evening, the walls were covered with vines and roses, and the kraals* were not made of red stone, but of lilac trees full of blossom. And the fat old Boer* smiled at her; and the stick he held across the door, for the goats to jump over, was a lily rod with seven blossoms at the end. When she went to the house her mistress gave her a whole roaster-cake for her supper, and the mistress's daughter had stuck a rose in the cake; and her mistress's son-in-law said, 'Thank you!' when she pulled off his boots, and did not kick her.

It was a beautiful dream.

While she lay thus dreaming, one of the little kids came and licked her on her cheek, because of the salt from her dried-up tears. And in her dream she was not a poor indentured child any more, living with Boers. It was her father who kissed her. He said he had only been asleep—that day when he lay down under the thorn-bush; he had not really died. He felt her hair, and said it was grown long and silky, and he said they would go back to Denmark now. He asked her why her feet were bare, and what the marks on her back were. Then he put her head on his shoulder, and picked her up, and carried her away, away! She laughed—she could feel her face against his brown beard. His arms were so strong.

As she lay there dreaming, with the ants running over her naked feet, and with her brown curls lying in the sand, a Hottentot* came up to her. He was dressed in ragged yellow trousers, and a dirty shirt, and torn jacket. He had a red handkerchief round his head, and a felt hat above that. His nose was flat, his eyes like slits, and the wool on his head was gathered into little round balls. He came to the milk-bush, and looked at the little girl lying in the hot sun. Then he walked off, and caught one of the fattest little Angora goats, and held its mouth fast, as he stuck it under his arm. He looked back to see that she was still sleeping, and jumped down into one of the sluits.* He walked down the bed of the sluit a little way and came to an overhanging bank, under which, sitting on the red sand, were two men. One was a tiny, ragged, old bushman, four feet high; the other was an English navvy, in a dark blue blouse. They cut the kid's throat with the navvy's long knife, and covered up the blood with sand, and buried the entrails and skin. Then they talked, and quarrelled a little; and then they talked quietly again.

The Hottentot man put a leg of the kid under his coat and left the rest of the meat for the two in the sluit, and walked away.

When little Jannita awoke it was almost sunset. She sat up very frightened, but her goats were all about her. She began to drive them home. 'I do not think there are any lost,' she said.

Dirk,* the Hottentot, had brought his flock home already, and stood at the kraal door with his ragged yellow trousers. The fat old Boer put his stick across the door, and let Jannita's goats jump over, one by one. He counted them. When the last jumped over: 'Have you been to sleep today?' he said; 'there is one missing.'

Then little Jannita knew what was coming, and she said, in a low voice, 'No.' And then she felt in her heart that deadly sickness that you feel when you tell a lie; and again she said, 'Yes.'

'Do you think you will have any supper this evening?' said the Boer.

'No,' said Jannita.

'What do you think you will have?'

'I don't know,' said Jannita.

'Give me your whip,' said the Boer to Dirk, the Hottentot.

The moon was all but full that night. Oh, but its light was beautiful!

The little girl crept to the door of the outhouse where she slept, and looked at it. When you are hungry, and very, very sore, you do not cry. She leaned her chin on one hand, and looked, with her great dove's eyes—the other hand was cut open, so she wrapped it in her pinafore. She looked across the plain at the sand and the low karoo-bushes, with the moonlight on them.

Presently, there came slowly, from far away, a wild springbuck. It came close to the house, and stood looking at it in wonder, while the moonlight glinted on its horns, and in its great eyes. It stood wondering at the red brick walls, and the girl watched it. Then, suddenly, as if it scorned it all, it curved its beautiful back and turned; and away it fled over the bushes and sand, like a sheeny streak of white lightning. She stood up to watch it. So free, so free! Away, away! She watched, till she could see it no more on the wide plain.

Her heart swelled, larger, larger, and larger: she uttered a low cry; and without waiting, pausing, thinking, she followed on its track. Away, away, away! 'I—I also!' she said, 'I—I also!'

When at last her legs began to tremble under her, and she stopped to breathe, the house was a speck behind her. She dropped on the earth, and held her panting sides.

She began to think now.

If she stayed on the plain they would trace her footsteps in the morning and catch her; but if she waded in the water in the bed of the river they would not be able to find her footmarks; and she would hide, there where the rocks and the kopjes* were.

So she stood up and walked towards the river. The water in the river was low; just a line of silver in the broad bed of sand, here and there broadening into a pool. She stepped into it, and bathed her feet in the delicious cold water. Up and up the stream she walked, where it rattled over the pebbles, and past where the farmhouse lay; and where the rocks were large she leaped from one to the other. The night wind in her face made her strong—she laughed. She had never felt such night wind before. So the night smells to the wild bucks, because they are free! A free thing feels as a chained thing never can.

At last she came to a place where the willows grew on each side of the river, and trailed their long branches on the sandy bed. She could not tell why, she could not tell the reason, but a feeling of fear came over her.

On the left bank rose a chain of kopjes and a precipice of rocks. Between the precipice and the river bank there was a narrow path covered by the fragments of fallen rock. And upon the summit of the precipice, a kippersol tree grew, whose palm-like leaves were clearly cut out against the night sky. The rocks cast a deep shadow, and the willow trees, on either side of the river. She paused, looked up and about her, and then ran on, fearful.

'What was I afraid of? How foolish I have been!' she said, when she came to a place where the trees were not so close together. And she stood still and looked back and shivered.

At last her steps grew wearier and wearier. She was very sleepy now, she could scarcely lift her feet. She stepped out of the river-bed. She only saw that the rocks about her were wild, as though many little kopjes had been broken up and strewn upon the ground, lay down at the foot of an aloe, and fell asleep.

But, in the morning, she saw what a glorious place it was. The rocks were piled on one another, and tossed this way and that. Prickly pears grew among them, and there were no less than six kippersol trees scattered here and there among the broken kopjes. In the rocks there were hundreds of homes for the conies,* and from the crevices wild asparagus* hung down. She ran to the river, bathed in the clear cold water, and tossed it over her head. She sang aloud. All the songs she knew were sad, so she could not sing them now, she was glad, she was so free; but she sang the notes without the words, as the cock-o-veets do. Singing and jumping all the way, she went back, and took a sharp stone, and cut at the root of a kippersol, and got out a large piece, as long as her arm, and sat to chew it. Two conies came out on the rock above her head and peeped at her. She held them out a piece, but they did not want it, and ran away.

It was very delicious to her. Kippersol is like

raw quince, when it is very green; but she liked it. When good food is thrown at you by other people, strange to say, it is very bitter; but whatever you find yourself is sweet!

When she had finished she dug out another piece, and went to look for a pantry to put it in. At the top of a heap of rocks up which she clambered,* she found that some large stones stood apart but met at the top, making a room.

'Oh, this is my little home!' she said.

At the top and all round it was closed, only in the front it was open. There was a beautiful shelf in the wall for the kippersol, and she scrambled down again. She brought a great bunch of prickly pear, and stuck it in a crevice before the door, and hung wild asparagus over it, till it looked as though it grew there. No one could see that there was a room there, for she left only a tiny opening, and hung a branch of feathery asparagus over it. Then she crept in to see how it looked. There was a glorious soft green light. Then she went out and picked some of those purple little ground flowers—you know them—those that keep their faces close to the ground, but when you turn them up and look at them they are deep blue eyes looking into yours! She took them with a little earth, and put them in the crevices between the rocks; and so the room was quite furnished. Afterwards she went down to the river and brought her arms full of willow, and made a lovely bed; and, because the weather was very hot, she lay down to rest upon it.

She went to sleep soon, and slept long, for she was very weak. Late in the afternoon she was awakened by a few cold drops falling on her face. She sat up. A great and fierce thunderstorm had been raging, and a few of the cool drops had fallen through the crevice in the rocks. She pushed the asparagus branch aside, and looked out, with her little hands folded about her knees. She heard the thunder rolling, and saw the red torrents rush among the stones on their way to the river. She heard the roar of the river as it now rolled, angry and red, bearing away stumps and trees on its muddy water. She listened and smiled, and pressed closer to the rock that took care of her. She pressed the palm of her hand against it. When you have no one to love you, you love the dumb things very much. When the sun set, it cleared up. Then the little girl ate some kippersol, and lay down again to sleep. She thought there was nothing so nice as to sleep. When one has had no food but kippersol juice for two days, one doesn't feel strong.

'It is so nice here,' she thought as she went to sleep, 'I will stay here always.'

Afterwards, the moon rose. The sky was very clear now, there was not a cloud anywhere; and the moon shone in through the bushes in the door, and made a lattice-work of light on her face. She was dreaming a beautiful dream. The loveliest dreams of all are dreamed when you are hungry. She thought she was walking in a beautiful place, holding her father's hand, and they both had crowns on their heads, crowns of wild asparagus. The people whom they passed smiled and kissed her; some gave her flowers, and some gave her food, and the sunlight was everywhere. She dreamed the same dream over and over, and it grew more and more beautiful; till, suddenly, it seemed as though she were standing quite alone. She looked up: on one side of her was the high precipice, on the other was the river, with the willow trees, drooping their branches into the water; and the moonlight was over all. Up, against the night sky the pointed leaves of the kippersol trees were clearly marked, and the rocks and the willow trees cast dark shadows.

In her sleep she shivered, and half awoke.

'Ah, I am not there, I am here,' she said; and she crept closer to the rock, and kissed it, and went to sleep again.

It must have been about three o'clock, for the moon had begun to sink towards the western sky, when she woke, with a violent start. She sat up, and pressed her hand against her heart.

'What can it be? A cony must surely have run across my feet and frightened me!' she said, and she turned to lie down again; but soon she sat up. Outside, there was the distinct sound of thorns crackling in a fire.

She crept to the door and made an opening in the branches with her fingers.

A large fire was blazing in the shadow, at the foot of the rocks. A little Bushman sat over some burning coals that had been raked from it, cooking meat. Stretched on the ground was an Englishman, dressed in a blouse, and with a heavy, sullen face. On the stone beside him was Dirk, the Hottentot, sharpening a bowie knife.

She held her breath. Not a cony in all the rocks was so still.

'They can never find me here,' she said; and she knelt, and listened to every word they said. She could hear it all.

'You may have all the money,' said the Bushman; 'but I want the cask of brandy. I will set the roof alight in six places, for a Dutchman burnt my mother once alive in a hut, with three children.'

'You are sure there is no one else on the farm?' said the Navvy.*

'No, I have told you till I am tired,' said Dirk; 'The two Kaffirs have gone with the son to town; and the maids have gone to a dance; there is only the old man and the two women left.'

'But suppose,' said the Navvy, 'he should have the gun at his bedside, and loaded!'

'He never has,' said Dirk; 'It hangs in the

passage, and the cartridges* too. He never thought when he bought it what work it was for! I only wish the little white girl was there still,' said Dirk; 'but she is drowned. We traced her footmarks to the great pool that has no bottom.'

She listened to every word, and they talked on.

Afterwards, the little Bushman, who crouched over the fire, sat up suddenly, listening.

'Ha! what is that?' he said.

A Bushman is like a dog: his ear is so fine he knows a jackal's tread from a wild dog's.

'I heard nothing,' said the Navvy.

'I heard,' said the Hottentot; 'but it was only a cony on the rocks.'

'No cony, no cony,' said the Bushman; 'see, what is that there moving in the shade round the point?'

'Nothing, you idiot!' said the Navvy. 'Finish your meat, we must start now.'

There were two roads to the homestead. One went along the open plain, and was by far the shortest; but you might be seen half a mile off. The other ran along the river bank, where there were rocks, and holes, and willow trees to hide among. And all down the river bank ran a little figure.

The river was swollen by the storm full to its banks, and the willow trees dipped their half-drowned branches into its water. Wherever there was a gap between them, you could see it flow, red and muddy, with the stumps upon it. But the little figure ran on and on; never looking, never thinking; panting, panting! There, where the rocks were the thickest; there, where on the open space the moonlight shone; there, where the prickly pears were tangled, and the rocks cast shadows, on it ran; the little hands clinched, the little heart beating, the eyes fixed always ahead.

It was not far to run now. Only the narrow path between the high rocks and the river.

At last she came to the end of it, and stood for an instant. Before her lay the plain, and the red farmhouse, so near, that if persons had been walking there you might have seen them in the moonlight. She clasped her hands. 'Yes, I will tell them, I will tell them!' she said; 'I am almost there!' She ran forward again, then hesitated. She shaded her eyes from the moonlight, and looked. Between her and the farmhouse there were three figures moving over the low bushes.

In the sheeny moonlight you could see how they moved on, slowly and furtively;* the short one, and the one in light clothes, and the one in dark.

'I cannot help them now!' she cried, and sank down on the ground, with her little hands clasped before her.

'Awake, awake!' said the farmer's wife; 'I hear a strange noise; something calling, calling, calling!'

The man rose, and went to the window.

'I hear it also,' he said, 'surely some jackal is at the sheep. I will load my gun and go and see.'

'It sounds to me like the cry of no jackal,' said the woman; and when he was gone she woke her daughter.

'Come, let us go and make a fire, I can sleep no more,' she said; 'I have heard a strange thing tonight. Your father said it was a jackal's cry, but no jackal cries so. It was a child's voice, and it cried, "Master, master, wake!"'

The women looked at each other; then they went to the kitchen, and made a great fire; and they sang psalms* all the while.

At last the man came back; and they asked him, 'What have you seen?' 'Nothing,' he said, 'but the sheep asleep in their kraals, and the moonlight on the walls. And yet, it did seem to me,' he added, 'that far away near the krantz* by the river, I saw three figures moving. And afterwards—it might have been fancy—I thought I heard the cry again; but since that, all has been still there.'

Next day, a Navvy had returned to the railway works.

'Where have you been so long?' his comrades asked.

'He keeps looking over his shoulder,' said one, 'as though he thought he should see something there.'

'When he drank his grog today,' said another, 'he let it fall, and looked round.'

Next day, a small old Bushman, and a Hottentot, in ragged yellow trousers, were at a wayside canteen. When the Bushman had had brandy, he began to tell how something (he did not say whether it was man, woman, or child) had lifted up its hands and cried for mercy; had kissed a white man's hands, and cried to him to help it. Then the Hottentot took the Bushman by the throat, and dragged him out.

Next night, the moon rose up and mounted the quiet sky. She was full now, and looked in at the little home; at the purple flowers stuck about the room, and the kippersol on the shelf. Her light fell on the willow trees, and on the high rocks, and on a little new-made heap of earth and round stones. Three men knew what was under it; and no one else ever will.

If you liked reading this story, you must also read:

The Story of an African Farm, The Woman's Rose, The Police in Favour of Protection

---

GLOSSARY:

Karoo: A type of shrub or a small to medium-sized tree that is native to southern Africa

Kraal: A traditional African village of huts, typically enclosed by a fence

Boer: Common name for Afrikaans-speaking white South Africans descended from the Dutch East India Company's original settlers at the Cape of Good Hope

Hottentot: A term that was historically used to refer to the Khoekhoe, the non-Bantu speaking indigenous nomadic pastoralists of South Africa

Sluits: A deep usually dry ditch produced by the washing of heavy rains in a large natural opening

Dirk: A long-bladed thrusting dagger

Kopjes: A small hill in a generally flat area

Conies: Rabbits

Asparagus: A low-calorie vegetable that is an excellent source of essential vitamins and minerals

Clambered: To climb or move in an awkward and laborious way using both hands and feet

Navvy: A labourer employed in construction

Cartridges: A type of pre-assembled firearm ammunition packaging a projectile

Furtively: To do something secretly

Psalms: A religious book in Christianity

Krantz: A sheer cliff or precipice in southern Africa

Mayy Ziyada, Egypt

(February 11, 1886 – October 17, 1941)

The Lebanese-Palestinian writer, Mayy Ziyada, is considered to have been a key figure of the Nahda[1] in the early twentieth-century Arab literary scene and deemed a pioneer of Oriental feminism.

Mayy Elias Ziyada was born to a Palestinian mother and a Lebanese father. Her mother was a mystical poet whereas her father was a school teacher. When she and her family relocated to Cairo, Egypt they entered an entirely different society, but it gave Ziyada a thriving opportunity to witness Egypt's feminist movements. From 1914 to the late 1920s, Ziyada was a significant player in Cairo's cultural life, hosting weekly salons attended by the greatest Arab intellectuals of the day.

A pioneer woman writer of fiction and poetry, she wrote quite extensively in French, and occasionally English or Italian, but as she matured, she increasingly found her literary voice in Arabic. She produced sixteen books, and even more articles, essays and short stories but these were not published in a book form until the 1920s, but soon she was published widely in Cairo and Beirut presses. She also corresponded intimately with the Arab-American writer, Gibran Khalil Gibran.

---

1 Nahda, also called the Awakening, is a cultural and intellectually reform movement that began in the late 19th and early 20th centuries in Egypt and then moved to Ottoman-ruled Arabic-speaking regions including Lebanon and Syria

The fact that Ziyada was an outsider to the Egyptian feminist movement was what made her so important. She was very aware that she was an outsider by religion and origin. However, she put her arguments in context with other feminist rhetoric and encouraged inclusiveness. Empathizing with others was the heart of her entire career as a writer. When she died in 1941, many of her works remained unpublished until the resurgence of her literature in the 1980s and 1990s.

In her lifetime, she produced various speeches, essays, prose poems, short stories, biographies of women, critical studies, and many translations from world literature, that resonated with her brilliance. Today, Ziyada is remembered because she paved the way for many women, inside and outside of her religion and origin by writing and thinking.

Woman with a Story

Every person has a special story. Relatives and distant relations tell it to each other in their various dialects; they understand it according to their different mentalities and weave a host of tales around it. Most often, one recounts the basic story about one's chosen victim, then adds, 'He played this trick on me!' and 'There was the saga with my colleague and that episode with someone else,' and so on. The narrator is lavish with this story, explaining it, going into great detail about it, embellishing it. And the others listen in amazement, tut-tutting and invoking the Almighty. They poke fun and jeer,* as if neither they nor anyone before them had ever done anything like what is being related to them. Naturally, when they apply the rules to others, they don't see how lax they are in judging themselves. Yet the golden principle of loving your neighbor and treating others as you wish to be treated yourself is still a golden principle. There's no getting away from it. When judging others, people don't follow the criteria they apply to themselves. They judge according to the rigid texts that make up the moral code, using these as ammunition against each other. If faults are put up for auction, it's an auction where competition to determine the lowest bidder is precluded. The speakers, whose capacity as such makes them righteous, pure, and saintly, turn to this severe code with the look of executioners. Just as the arithmetic table that the Greek Pythagoras invented provides us with a ready reckoner, so the moral code provides us with a way of reckoning up the evil deeds of God's servants and judging them. It's a ready reckoner whose sublime numerals are above any dubious deduction!

I used to encounter Madame Gh B frequently in various places: at church, at concerts, and in department stores. I rarely walked through the streets of the Ismailiyya quarter, such as Qasr al-Nil, Imad al-Din, al-Maghribi, al-Madabigh, and Sulayman Pasha, without seeing her pass by so that it seemed she must live in one of these districts or nearby. If I was with a friend or companion, up would go the cry that women usually utter—and men too, with due respect to our honorable gentlemen—when a woman with some distinguishing feature passes by: 'Look! Look!' And Madame Gh B had more than one distinguishing feature. She was known for her beautiful voice—I heard her sing at two concerts—and she dressed elegantly, in the most up-to-date clothes. In fact, she was among the first to popularize the latest fashions in Cairo. And she was known as a beauty.

I used to watch her from a distance, attracted to her by that special thing that is in all human beings. It's not their clothes, or their facial features, or the way they move, or their silence; it's something indefinable, something that differs with each individual. Some observers of physiognomy* maintain that it's located between the eyes; others say it's in the pupil of the eye, or around the mouth, or in the line of the lips, or in the tilt of the chin. I only know that it's there and that it's the greatest definer of what we call the individual's 'personality.' With some people, it's very strong and has a great impact. It seizes the onlookers, and after that, they can never forget this personality or its possessor.

Once the words 'Look! Look!' have been uttered, there inevitably follows a story about the subject under scrutiny. That's how I came to hear many stories about Madame Gh B, stories that made me think a lot about her. I wondered what she was really like. What should I believe from all the gossip? My preoccupation with her increased as the stories about her mounted. I was like the man who was introduced to a celebrity and said, 'I've heard all the bad things people say about you, and I couldn't wait to get to know such a formidable person.'

Her eyes were the thing that stuck most firmly in my mind. They were ever-changing. Sometimes they looked like the eyes of a woman in pain, a long-suffering woman; and sometimes they were contemplative, avoiding all the show of life. Sometimes they had an unfathomable* look: they stared straight ahead, piercing through objects into space as if watching the signs of an invisible hand in the air. And sometimes they seemed like the eyes of a gregarious person who enjoys the usual festivities and is quite content with them, not imagining that anything better exists. At these times they shone, happy, as if life had given them their fill of quiet delight, and was realizing its highest hopes through them. But I liked them when they became dull and the light in them went out as if she had aged fifty years in two weeks. Then I would meet her another time, and in her rose-colored dress, with her hat fluttering around her face, she would seem like a child, anticipating all sorts of joys from life.

One day the cream of the city's amateur musicians gave a concert in the big festival hall at the Shepherd Hotel. Two famous instructors supervised the organization of the concert. One was Mrs K, the most talented of the foreign singing teachers. She held recitals at her home, and those who studied under her and moved in her circle—the finest singers of Cairo—flocked to them. The other was Signore F, who had lived in the city for years and had numerous students from various colonies of foreigners. He regularly performed such miracles on the piano that the number of his friends and admirers grew steadily.

At this concert, Madame Gh B sang. But, I couldn't find anyone who could tell me anything about her—perhaps because most of the people present were amateurs. Every time a performer played, or a singer sang, they all rushed to congratulate his or her relatives, thus guaranteeing that they would also be congratulated when their children sang and played. The woman didn't have any family, yet her singing created a big stir and provoked loud applause, which she accepted with simple silence. A deep, jet-black flame appeared in her eyes; she had the look of a woman who was neither young nor old, like a statue, with unchanging features and unvarying posture.

I thought about her for a long time that evening, and from all that I had heard about her, I pieced together a sad story. I said to myself, 'What a waste! Why does this woman pretend not to know her true self? Why doesn't she forget she's beautiful and rise to the level I'm sure she merits?'

The following morning, Signore F came to give me my piano lesson. Instead of arriving at eleven o'clock, which was the appointed time, he arrived at ten minutes to noon. He came in, rubbing his hands, his eyes shining behind his glasses. I grumbled, 'Signore, you don't care about my time! You've ruined my morning. In fact, you've ruined my entire day!'

He laughed; it was a laugh that began moderately but ended in a sound like the chirping of birds. 'I'm not a mathematics teacher,' he said. 'I'm not obliged to come at the appointed time.' And he rubbed his hands again, citing a French proverb to the effect that some confusion is necessary for the enhancement of art.

'But my time—' I said. He interrupted me, 'The lesson! The lesson!' And so for a long hour, the neighbors were treated to that special noise of a student practicing and repeating as the teacher looks on.

When the hour came to an end, and the labors were over and peace restored, I demanded my due. If Signore F was satisfied with his students, he would play whatever they requested. The reward I requested that day was a piece of Russian music that he had played the previous day.

He sat at the piano, and before he started

playing, we talked about the concert and exchanged views about the voices of the singers, eventually arriving at Madame Gh B.

'Is she one of your students?' I asked.

'No, no. She's one of Mrs K's students. She's been to her house several times.'

'Sometimes they call her Madame and sometimes Mademoiselle. Is she married or single?'

He sighed and said, 'Poor woman!'

'What's so terrible about her life that it makes you feel so sorry for her?'

'Who wouldn't feel sorry for a woman who has beauty, intelligence, and goodness, who's been given everything she needs to be happy, and yet has had nothing but misery in life?'

'What misery?'

'What? Don't you know her story?'

'I know little bits here and there. You can't really get a clear picture of someone's life from what people say.'

He sighed again, and his fingertips hurried over the musical scale, as if he were releasing some of his grief, or looking for a new way to tell an old story. Then his expression clouded, and he said,

'Her father was a judge in the mixed courts. He was very learned and intelligent, so he taught his daughter and gave her the best education. When the time came for her to be married, the same thing happened to her as happens to a lot of girls.

Her parents chose a fiancé for her, a foreigner, and she had no say about him. The fiancé was quite handsome, so she didn't object. She was content, like many of her sisters, to receive the customary gifts of clothes and jewelry, and to attain a certain measure of freedom and independence. So she was married and had a magnificent wedding, to which the most prominent people from the European colonies were invited. It wasn't long before the husband claimed what had been agreed as a dowry.'

Signore F stopped talking. A look of mingled shame, compassion, and contempt clouded his face. After a moment of silence, he continued, 'Many women make men unhappy. Many women tear marriages apart and break people's hearts. But if a woman is not a wicked person, then she's really unfortunate. However much she rises up in her own eyes, however much she's liberated from her chains, and however much those who defend her rights exaggerate in raising her to a man's level, her life, her entire life, remains in the grip of this being—this man—whose equal she claims to be. In reality, she's nothing but what he wants her to be. If he's free and noble, he makes her free and noble. If he's low and mean, he debases and humiliates her. She's his plaything; she's his slave; something he need show no restraint with, whatever the situation. Men who have a conscience are frightened by this authority over women, this power. It's a power that scoffs* at changes in politics and society because it's stronger than either of them and more deeply rooted—in nature itself. So they refrain from marrying out of fear of themselves.'

His comments were important, but they irritated me—I wanted to hear the rest of the story. So I said, 'Then what happened?'

'What happened is that this imposter had a secret relationship with another woman and needed money, and marriage was the easiest way to get it. After three weeks, he disappeared.'

'How did he disappear?'

'He left the house and never returned. For the first few days, his wife went mad, thinking he had died. Weeks went by and the news that he had gone off with his first wife started to spread. So they sent people out to look for him in his own country, Italy'—and here Signore F swallowed hard because he was Italian—'but the efforts of the police were in vain. They found no trace of him, either in Italy or in any other country in the West. Shortly after that, the father of this woman, who'd been cheated out of her youth, love, money, and standing, had died. She became lonely and poor. The church refused to annul her marriage because the man hadn't married his first wife in church; it was a marriage by agreement only. There's a legal penalty for this, but how can the law reach someone who's vanished? Even if the church annulled* the woman's marriage, people would still have their suspicions about her, because the one who's wronged is more vulnerable to suspicions and speculations than the wrongdoer, especially if the wronged person is a woman and the wrongdoer is a man. That's why people watch every move she makes. She's settled on their tongues and become a tasty morsel* for their chitchat. Even if she were to spend her days fasting, praying, and living the life of an ascetic,* they wouldn't give her her due. No matter how high a price she paid them, they wouldn't sell her that illusory regard with which they flatter people of power and wealth and authority or those who are good at duping them. What purpose does this woman have in life? She's not divorced, so she isn't free to spend her time as she wants, and she isn't chained, so she can't console herself by breaking her chains. It's a crippled sort of life. The man made her miserable, just as he has crippled many other women before her and made them miserable.'

'But how is it that she didn't see through his deception during the engagement?'

'I don't know why she didn't realize. And her family didn't notice anything either.'

'Perhaps he was sincere when he married her, but kept thinking of the other woman. Perhaps she was very beautiful.'

'Those who know her say she's an old gray-haired woman and are amazed that this bright, elegant man should be content with her—even as a servant.' Signore F lowered his head and remained silent for a while. Then he continued, 'But youth and beauty don't have any bearing on these matters. People look for beauty in the salon, in the theater, in society, and on the street, and a pretty woman usually attracts more attention than a plain one. But the effect of her looks doesn't go beyond this—history proves my point. The most recent historical example is that of the crown prince of Austria, whose murder set off World War I. He was the one who turned away from all the Austrian archduchesses and their dazzling beauty, and rejected all the princesses in the ruling dynasties, and abdicated* from the throne and the crown to marry a woman who was the least graceful and beautiful of all. That was the Countess Sophia Chotek, a lady-in-waiting to one of his female relatives. After her marriage, she became the Duchess of Hohenberg, and was killed with him in the tragic incident at Sarajevo.'

Signore F settled himself in his seat and began to play a sad, stirring piece by Beethoven: The Funeral March of the *Eroica* Symphony.

Yesterday in a garden on the outskirts of Cairo, I saw the woman with the story. I understand now why the expression in her eyes changes. While I don't yet fully understand what the words 'crippled life' mean, I do realize that life prepares circumstances for some people that they never dreamed of, and if they were to dream of them, they would try to eliminate them, even if it meant walking on thorns and burning coals. I have learned that in that upright figure, in that body which expresses strength and pride, there is a heart once wounded by true love. But today it is tortured by a cancer with roots spreading to all its corners, that deep-seated cancer which cannot be eradicated: contempt for life and lack of trust in people.

If you liked reading this story, you must also read:
Platters of Crumbs, Words and Signs, The Meaning of Life

GLOSSARY:

Jeer: Make rude and mocking remarks

Physiognomy: The practice of assessing a person's character or personality from their outer appearance, especially the face

Unfathomable: Incapable of being fully explored or understood

Scoffs: To speak to someone or about something in a derisive or mocking way
Annulled: To declare an official document or marriage invalid
Morsel: A small piece or amount of food
Ascetic: To be practising strict self-denial as a measure of personal and especially spiritual discipline
Abdicated: Renounce from one's throne or resign from a position

---

Our gratitude to State University of New York Press for letting us use this story.
Mayy Ziyada, Cohen-Mor, Dalya, Arab Women Writers: An Anthology of Short Stories, State University of New York Press, 2005

Ryunosuke Akūtagawa, Japan

(March 1, 1892 – July 24, 1927)

The Japanese writer, Ryunosuke Akūtagawa, is regarded as the Father of the Japanese short story. Akūtagawa wrote in the Japanese language and is especially known for his stories based on Japanese past and for his stylistic virtuosity with which he re-tells that history.

Akūtagawa was ill and hypersensitive as a child, although he excelled in school and was an avid reader. He began his literary career while attending, what is now called the University of Tokyo. He studied English literature for three years.

The publication of his short story *Rashōmon* in 1915 led to his meeting with Natsume Sōseki, the best Japanese novelist of the day. With Sōseki's support, he began to compose a series of stories based mostly on collections of Japanese tales from the twelfth and thirteenth centuries but reinterpreted in the light of modern psychology and a very distinctive style. He drew inspiration from a wide range of sources, including China, Japan's sixteenth-century Christian community in Nagasaki, and European relations with nineteenth-century Japan. Many of his pieces are written with a feverish intensity that matches their frequently terrible subjects.

Kappa (1927), a satiric fable about elflike creatures (kappa), is written in the mirthless tone of his final years and depicts his unhappy attitude at the time. In 1927, the literary community was taken aback by his suicide.

Today, Aktagawa is one of Japan's most widely translated authors, and several of his works have been adapted for films. *Rashomon* (1950) is based on Aktagawa's stories. The Aktagawa Prize, Japan's highest literary honour, is also named after him.

The Nose

If you mention 'the Nose,' that high-ranking priest from Zenchi Temple, you won't find a soul in Ikenō* who doesn't know the name. Five or six inches long, it hung down from above his upper lip down to the bottom of his chin. Its width was the same from top to bottom. To get a good picture of it, imagine someone with a long, thin sausage dangling casually down the middle of his face.

This Buddhist priest was now in his fifties. From the time he was an apprentice in the inner hall, climbing the ranks, even until the present day, he was constantly worrying about his nose. Of course, during all this time, he continued to pretend that he didn't care about it in the least. It wasn't just that as a monk he should've been completely focused on the Pure Land awaiting him in the afterlife, it was that he didn't want other people to know he was so concerned about his nose. Nothing terrified him more than the idea that someone would bring up his nose in conversation.

There were two reasons why he found his nose to be so burdensome. The first was that a long nose, practically speaking, was not very useful. He couldn't even eat breakfast by himself. If he tried to eat alone, the tip of his nose would poke into the middle of the food in his bowl. So the Nose had one of the apprentice* monks sit a few feet across from him and hold up his nose.

But eating this way was no simple task, not for the Nose, and not for the assisting apprentice. One time, a temple pageboy was substituted for the usual apprentice monk, and when this young man sneezed, he accidentally shook his hand, and the Nose's nose ended up thrust into the middle of his rice gruel,* at least according to the rumor going around Kyoto in those days. Still, in spite of all that, that's not what really bothered the Nose. What really worried him was the damage to his self-esteem.

As for the people in Ikenō, they maintained that they were happy to have someone with such a nose, such a holy priest at Zenchi Temple. This was because, with that nose, they thought no girl would marry him. Between themselves, they reasoned that his nose was the only reason he became a monk in the first place. But for the Nose, the mere fact of being a monk didn't make him feel any less burdened by his nose. He felt like he was married to the strain this nose had placed upon him, and this was a delicate situation for him. Because of this, he tried passively, actively, to restore his damaged self-esteem in any way that he could.

The first thing that came to mind was to find a way to make his nose look shorter than it really was. When nobody was around, he'd sit in front of the mirror, experimenting with various lighting schemes, zealously* laboring to hold different poses. No matter how he tried positioning his face, he was never satisfied, sitting there with his head propped on his hands and his fingers on his chin, spending hours peeking diligently into the mirror.

However, he never once found a way to make his nose appear shorter. At times, it worried him to the point where he thought his nose actually looked longer. Shutting away his mirror in a box, he'd breathe a heavy sigh and go reluctantly to his sutra-reading desk and read Kannon's prayer until he fell asleep.

From this point on, he was constantly aware of other peoples' noses. The monks at the temple in Ikenō often begged for alms,* had lectures, and so on. The temple interior was connected directly to a bathhouse, and the monks boiled water every day. Consequently, many kinds of monks could be seen there, coming and going. The Nose patiently scanned the faces of the various people. He wanted to find someone with a nose like his own, thinking this would put him at ease. Because of this, in his eyes, people weren't wearing navy blue robes or white morning kimonos, not to mention things like orange hats or dull priests' robes. He was accustomed to seeing these things, but it was all the same to him; he didn't see people, only their noses. However, even though he saw hooked noses, he didn't see a single nose that resembled his own. Not being able to find another nose like his, this weighed heavily upon him, and once again, he became despondent. While talking to people, he would aimlessly pinch the tip of his own nose, blush as if he'd forgotten his age, and then feel supremely unhappy about his own behavior.

Finally, he decided to search through the mounds of Buddhist and non-Buddhist literature, to try and discover a personage with a nose like his own, which he thought would lighten his spirits somewhat.

But it turned out that there was nothing in the sutras concerning whether Maudgayayana and his ilk or figures such as Sariputra had long noses. Naturally, Nagarjuna and Asvaghosa, bodhisattvas, were furnished with nice, ordinary noses. When the Nose heard that Liu Xuande, founder of the

Shu-Han dynasty in ancient China, had had long ears, he wondered if it were his nose that was long, would his own feelings of helplessness have been lessened at all.

While part of him was feeling this passive anxiety, another part of him was actively trying to find ways to make his nose shorter, almost too many to mention here. To this end, he tried everything he could. He'd tried drinking a boiled concoction* from a snake gourd, he tried rubbing rat piss onto his nose. However, no matter what he tried, he'd be damned if his nose wasn't the same as ever: five or six inches long, hanging down from above his upper lip.

But one autumn, the apprentice monk helping the Nose had gone on a visit to the capital, where he learnt from an acquaintance of his, a doctor, a method for making noses shorter. This doctor, he came over from China and became a monk in Chōrakuji Temple.

The Nose, acting disinterested as usual about anything having to do with noses, did what he could to pretend he didn't want to run out and try this new method. Then someone else, in a carefree tone, mentioned that it must be a burden for the apprentice having to help the Nose every time he ate, and this was a terrible blow. Of course, the young monk wouldn't say so, but he, too, was eager to try out the method. This young monk, and the Nose as well, it's doubtful that either one was unaware of the baiting that had occurred.

However, more than his opposition, more than avoiding this obvious trick, there was the fact of the Nose's sympathy for this poor apprentice who had to hold up his nose. The apprentice monk, as the Nose expected, blurted out his opinion that they try it out. So the Nose, as he'd known all along that he would, eventually gave in and decided to follow the recommendation that was so enthusiastically proffered.*

The method in question put simply, was to boil the nose with hot water and then have someone stomp on it. An extremely simple procedure, so to speak.

Every day, hot water was boiled in the temple's hot bath. From there, the apprentice brought back a bucket filled with water too hot to even dip a finger in. But they both feared that if the Nose were to dip his nose right into it, his face would be scalded by the hot steam. So they decided to bore a hole into a wooden tray and use it to cover the bucket. The Nose could stick his nose into the hole. Just dipping his nose into the hot water, it wouldn't be so bad.

'Let's start right away,' said the apprentice monk…let us cut to right after they boiled it.

The Nose gave a bitter smile. Having heard only about his nose, he felt that soon nobody would recognize him. With his nose soaking in the hot water, it was as itchy as if it were being eaten up by fleas.

When he pulled his nose out from the hole in the bucket's cover, it was still dripping from the steam. The apprentice began stomping on it hard with each of his feet. The Nose was lying on his side, with his nose protruding out onto the floorboards, watching the apprentice's feet go up and down in front of his eyes.

The apprentice monk, casting a pitiful glance down upon the Nose's bald head said:

'It probably hurts, doesn't it? The doctor blames the stomping for that. Anyway, it probably hurts.'

The Nose shook his head as if to say it didn't hurt. Anyway, he didn't shake his head like his nose was being stomped on. Then he looked up at the apprentice's cracked feet and said, angrily:

'I said it doesn't hurt!'

In reality, the apprentice was stomping on the spots where his nose itched, so rather than hurting, it almost did feel good.

After being stomped on for a while, before long, spots that looked like grains of millet started to appear on the nose. It looked like a bird whose feathers had been plucked and was now ready for roasting. The apprentice stopped stomping and said, as if to himself:

'He said to pluck these out with tweezers.'

The Nose puffed his cheeks as if he were short of breath, and waited silently for the apprentice to continue. Of course, it wasn't that he couldn't tell that the young monk was trying to help.

He knew that. But it was his nose that was being manhandled, so he was forced to focus on his own discomfort. The Nose made a face like a patient who doesn't trust the doctor doing surgery on him, and he watched as pus oozed from the pores in his nose being squeezed open by the tweezers. The pus looked like the quills of bird feathers, and almost one-fourth as long.

After a while, when this part was finished, the apprentice monk heaved a sigh of relief and said:

'And now, we boil it again.'

The Nose looked battered. With his nose still in a boomerang shape, he nodded.

Then, after they boiled it a second time and took it out of the water to check, it had, in fact, become shorter than it was. It didn't look so different from an ordinary hooked nose. Stroking his nose, the Nose peered bashfully into the mirror that the apprentice produced.

That nose—the one that before had hung down past his chin—he couldn't believe it was this short, the idea that he would've had to live the rest of his life without self-respect seemed like a lie. Still speckled* here and there, this was probably just the aftereffect of having been stomped on. Make no mistake, people won't sneer at a nose like this. The face of the Nose in the mirror shot a satisfied wink at the Nose outside of the mirror.

Nevertheless, that same day, he grew uneasy, wondering if his nose wouldn't grow long again. To that end, while reading the sutras, even while eating, in every spare moment, he would pull out his hand and gently touch his nose. But, his well-mannered nose was settled into place above his top lip, giving no indication that it was going to return to its previous dangling state. After that, he slept through the night, and waking up early the next morning, the first thing he did was touch his nose. It was as short as it was before. With that, he felt as elated as if he'd spent years copying the Lotus Sutra and accumulating good karma.

Still, over the next two or three days, the Nose made an unexpected discovery. It started with a bureaucrat* visiting Ikenō temple, who, even more than before, made a strange face upon seeing the Nose. He was rendered speechless, his eyes transfixed on the Nose's face. Outside the lecture hall, the Nose walked past some temple pageboys familiar with the rice gruel incident. As he walked by them, they looked down and restrained themselves, but finally, a laugh escaped. The second rate teachers called for order, talking to the Nose respectfully, but as soon as he turned away, they also burst into laughter. This happened more than just once or twice.

At first, the Nose reasoned that they behaved this way because his face had changed. However, this explanation only satisfied him for about ten minutes. Of course, what caused the pageboys and the crummy teachers to laugh was his face, no two ways about it.

Still, even though they laughed before, when his nose was long, the way they laughed was now somehow different. While they were used to seeing his nose long before, now they were more amused by his ridiculous short nose. But it still seemed like there was something more to it: they didn't laugh like that before.

The Nose finished reciting his sutras, and while tilting his head to one side, he would sometimes mutter to himself. The Nose, who should love everyone, when things got like that, without thinking, he stared at the figure of Samantabhadra on his white elephant, and, remembering the long nose he'd had four or five days before, he said, 'People who fall from grace long for the days of their former glory,' and he shut his mouth. The Nose regretfully reached an illuminating conclusion:

In the hearts of people, there are two conflicting interests. Of course, anybody can sympathize with the misfortune of another. However, when another person can somehow overcome his misfortune, we feel unsatisfied. To exaggerate just a little, we wish for that person to regain his misfortune once more. We usually feel ambiguous about this, but, on occasion, they embrace a certain animosity towards that person.

The Nose, still not knowing the reason why, felt perturbed. He realized the Ikenō monks' behavior was nothing more than a reflection of their own selfishness.

After that, the Nose's spirits grew darker each day. Surrounded by irritating gossip, he was nastily scolding everybody. Finally, he overheard that the very apprentice monk who'd helped with his treatment was saying, 'The Nose is committing the sin of jealousy.'

Another thing that upset the Nose was something one of the temple pageboys did. One day, the Nose heard a dog howling. He strolled out to investigate and saw a pageboy, brandishing* a twig about two feet long, running around chasing a skinny, shaggy dog. He wasn't just chasing it; 'Hit you with my nose! Hit you with my nose!' he shouted as he ran. The Nose plucked the stick from his hand and smacked him across the face with it. It was the most disgusting looking stick imaginable, from a rotting tree.

The Nose was resentful. Not that his nose used to be long, but because it was now short.

One evening, after the sun had set, the wind

started blowing, causing the bells in the pagoda to ring fiercely, and the monks to toss and turn atop their pillows. What's more, the wind was remarkably cold, and the Nose, the old man that he was, tried to sleep, but sleep just wouldn't come. He stared up from his bed, and after a short while, he realized his nose was itching. Touching it with his fingers, it felt moist and started to swell a little. There was nothing he could do; it seemed he'd caught a fever.

'Making my nose short is probably why I got sick,' he muttered, touching his nose as reverently as if he were offering incense in front of a statue of Buddha.

The next morning, the Nose woke up early, as usual, and the ginkgo trees and horse chestnut trees covering the temple grounds had all dropped their leaves overnight. The yard was bright as if someone had carpeted it with gold. This was probably due to the frost covering the rooftops nearby. In the thin morning light, the rings adorning the zenith of the pagoda shined brilliantly. The monks of Zenchi Temple lifted the shutters covering the porch, and deeply inhaled the morning air.

This is when, as if he had forgotten, he first realized that a certain sensation had returned.

The Nose, in confusion, lifted his hand to his nose. The thing he touched, was not the short nose of the night before. From above his upper lip to the bottom of his chin, four or five inches long, it hung down. It was the long nose he'd had before. In the course of one night, his nose had returned to its former length. He felt just as cheerful as he was when his nose became short, he felt that his nose had come back to him.

After this, I'm certain nobody will laugh, is what the Nose felt in his heart. His long nose was blown about by the first winds of autumn.

If you liked reading this story, you must also read:

Old Age, The Handkerchief, Tobacco and the Devil

GLOSSARY:

Ikenō: A local area in the Ikeda, Ibi District of Gifu, Japan

Apprentice: A person who is learning a trade from a skilled employer

Gruel: A thin liquid food of oatmeal or other meal boiled in milk or water

Zealously: With great energy or enthusiasm in pursuit of a cause or objective
Alms: Charity or money or food given to poor people
Concoction: A mixture of various ingredients or elements
Proffered: To offer or put forward something
Speckled: Covered or marked with a large number of small spots or patches of colour
Bureaucrat: An official in a government department
Brandishing: Wave or flourish something as a threat, in anger or excitement

Horacio Quiroga, Uruguay

(December 31, 1878 – February 19, 1937)

The Uruguayan writer, Horacio Quiroga, is considered to be the father of the Latin American short story. He wrote in Spanish and as a well-known poet and playwright, many of his writings were successful even during his lifetime. His evocative depiction of humans and animals struggling to survive in the tropical rainforest won him the reputation as the master of the short story. He also excelled at expressing mental illness and hallucination* states in writings that foreshadowed those of subsequent twentieth-century masters like the American writer, William Faulkner.

Horacio Silvestre Quiroga Forteza's life was plagued with tragedies, suicides, and early deaths, and these experiences inspire varied elements in his works. After travels in Europe during his youth, Quiroga spent most of his life in Buenos Aires and took frequent trips to the jungle province of Misiones, which provided the material for most of his stories.

During his entire life, Quiroga was attracted again and again to the jungle and lived in Misiones for long periods. His most famous stories take place in these locations and depict man's impotence against nature's violent horror. This reflects in his early works like the collection of prose and verse, *The Coral Reefs* (1901).

Quiroga found his direction in the short story and recognized Edgar Allan Poe as a major influence on his work. He was also influenced by Guy de Maupassant and Rudyard Kipling. In and beyond the Spanish-speaking world, he is still much admired today and looked up to for his invention of the Latin American short story.

The Son

It's a rough summer morning in Misiones, with all the sun, heat and tranquility* that the season can provide. Mother Nature, open to the skies, seems proud of herself.

Like the sun, the heat, and the tranquil atmosphere, the father opens his heart to nature.

'Be careful, little one.' He says to his son, summarizing in one phrase all of the observations of what could go wrong, and his son understanding perfectly.

'Yes, papa.' Responds the young child, while picking up the shotgun and filling his shirt pockets with cartridges, buttoning them closed carefully.

'Come back at lunchtime.' The father adds.

'Yes, papa.' The boy repeats.

He balances the shotgun in his hand, smiles at his father, kisses him on the head and leaves.

His father follows him a bit with his eyes and goes back to his daily chores, gleaming with joy over his young one.

He knows that his son, taught from the youngest age proper habit and precaution when dealing in danger, can handle a firearm and hunt whatever he wishes. Even though he is very tall for his age, he's only thirteen. And judging by his pure blue eyes, still sparkling with infantile* joy, he looks even younger.

The father doesn't even have to raise his head from his chores to follow his son's path: already across the reddened path and walking upright to the forest past the opening in the grass field.

In order to hunt in the forest—a game hunt—one needs more patience than his young son can muster. After crossing the island of trees, the boy will follow the line of cactuses towards the marshland*, looking for doves, toucans*, or any kind of heron, like those that his friend Juan had discovered a few days back.

Now alone, the father smirks recalling the passion for hunting that young children share. At times they would hunt a yacu-toro* or—if lucky—a surucua* and return triumphant. Juan to his ranch with his nine-millimetre firearm that had been given to him, and his son to the plateau with his huge, sixteen caliber, white powder, four lock Saint-Etienne shotgun.

The father had been the same. At thirteen, he would have given his life for a shotgun. His son, at the same age, now had one; and his father smiled.

Nevertheless, it is not easy for a widowed father, who without any other faith or hope in life other than his son, to educate his son like he had been taught, free in his limited range of knowledge, confident in his tiny feet and hands since four years old, conscious of the immensity of certain dangers and the scarcity of his own strengths.

This father had fought hard against what he sees as his own selfishness. It's so easy for a child to miscalculatc, put a foot in an empty hole and one loses a son.

Danger can always linger for a man despite his age, but the threat diminished since at an early age, he learned to count on nothing besides his own abilities.

This is how the father had raised his son. And to achieve it he had to resist not only his heart but his moral torments as well; because this father, of the weak stomach and poor eyesight, has for some time suffered from hallucinations.

He has seen, in painfully clear visions, memories of happiness that should have remained in the void where he has locked himself. The image of his own son has not escaped his torment. He had once seen him rolling, covered in blood, from hammering a parabellum* bullet in the vice in his workshop; he had felt this despite that his son was only polishing his belt buckle.

Horrible things...But today, with the burning summer day full of life, the love of which his son seems to have inherited, the father feels happy, calm and sure of the future.

In that moment, not far off, he hears a loud boom.

'The Saint Etienne,' the father thinks recognizing the detonation. Two fewer doves in the forest.

Without paying any more attention to the menial* event, the man distracts himself with his work.

The sun, already very high, continues to rise. Wherever one looks—rocks, earth, trees—, the air, congested like an oven, vibrates with heat. A deep humming sound fills the entire body and saturates the atmosphere for as far as the eyes can see, a time that harnesses all tropical life.

The father takes a look at his wristwatch: twelve. And lifts his eyes out over the forest.

His son should already be back. In the mutual trust that the two give to one another—the father of silvery sideburns and the child of thirteen—there were never any lies. When his son said, 'yes, papa,' he did what he was told. He said he would be back before twelve, and the father had smiled watching him leave.

But he hasn't come back.

The father returns to his chores, struggling to concentrate on his work. It's so easy, so easy to lose track of time when inside the forest, sitting a bit on the ground while resting motionless.

Suddenly, the midday sun, the tropical humming, and the beating of father's heart stop in rhythm at the thought: his son, motionless...

Time has passed; twelve-thirty. The father leaves his workshop, and resting his hand on the metal bench, the explosion of a parabellum bullet rushes from the depth of his memory, and instantly, for the first time in the last three hours, realizes that he has not heard a sound after the blast of the Saint-Etienne. He has not heard gravel stirring under familiar steps. His son hasn't returned, and nature stands guard at the edge of the forest, awaiting him.

Oh, how the calm character and young confidence of the boy's education is not enough to scare away the fatal ghost that the hallucinating father sees rising from the edge of the forest. Distraction, forgetfulness, fortuitous tardiness: none of these minute motives that could have delayed the arrival of his son could fit into the father's heart.

A shot, he had heard one single shot, and a

long time ago at that. Since then the father has not heard a single noise, has not seen a single bird, not a single person has walked through the opening in the grass field to announce that at the wire fence...a great disaster.

Distracted and without a machete,* the father sets out. He cuts through the grass field, enters into the forest, follows the line of cactus without finding the slightest trace of his son.

Nature continues to stand still. And when the father had gone over all of the familiar hunting paths and had explored the marshlands in vain, he knew with certainty that each step forward would bring him, relentlessly and brutally, to the body of his son.

He could only blame himself, poor thing. There was only the cold reality, terrible and consuming: his son had died crossing a...

But where, in what field? There are so many fences, and the forest is so, so, muddy. God, so muddy. If one is not careful crossing the fences with the shotgun in their hand...

The father's shout is stifled.* He saw something rise into the air, oh, no, no it's not his son...He turns to one direction, then the other, then the other.

Nothing could be gained by seeing the complexion of the man's skin and the anguish in his eyes. The father still hasn't called out to his son.

Even though his heart yearns to shout, his mouth remains shut. He knows well that the simple act of pronouncing his name, calling out to him loudly, would be a confession of his death.

'*Chiquito**' he let out quickly. And if the voice of a principled was capable of crying, we would cover our ears with compassion from the anguish in his voice.

No one nor nothing responded. Down the sun-reddened paths, the father, who has aged ten years by now, went searching for his newly-dead son.

'*Hijito mio*!'*...'*Chiquito mio**'...he clamored to his son in diminutives* that rose from the depths of his soul.

Once before, in the throngs of happiness and peace, this father suffered the hallucination of his son rolling on the ground, his head opened by a chrome-nickel bullet. Now, in every shadowed corner of the forest, he sees sparkling wires, and at the base of a post, with the discharged shotgun as his side, he sees his son.

'Sonny'...'my boy!'

Even the forces that bring a father to hallucinate the most awful of nightmares have their limits. The father feels his senses leaving him when he quickly sees his son stepping out from a side path.

From fifty meters, it was enough for the boy of thirteen to see his father's expression, without a machete and in the forest, to make him hurry his steps with his eyes wet.

'Son,' the man murmured. Exhausted, the man drops himself into the bright white sand, his hands clasped around his son's legs.

The young one, with his legs, hugged tightly, stands up, and understanding the pain of his father, caresses his head slowly.

'Poor, papa.'

More time has passed. It's already close to three. Now together, father and son undertake the walk back to the house.

'Why didn't you use the sun to keep track of time?' The father says first.

'I did, papa...but when I was headed back I saw the Garzas* that Juan caught and went after them.'

'What you put me through, son!'

'*Pia pia*,'* the boy murmurs back.

After a long silence, the father asks,

'And the Garzas, did you kill any?'

'No.'

Considering everything, a minute detail. Under the red hot sky, passing through the grass field, the man returns to his house with his son, on whose shoulders, almost even with his father's, he carries the joyful arm of his father. He returns covered in sweat, and even broken in body and spirit, smiles with joy.....

Yet he smiles a hallucinated happiness...For

this father walks alone. He has encountered no one, his arm supported by nothing but air. Because behind him, at the foot of a post and with his legs raised, tangled in barbed-wire, his loved son lies face down to the sun, dead since ten that morning.

If you liked reading this story, you must also read:

The Feather Pillow, The Yabebirí Pass, The Lazy Bee

GLOSSARY:

Hallucination: A perception of having seen, heard, touched, tasted or smelled something that wasn't actually there

Tranquillity: To be in a state of calm and peace

Infantile: Childish or juvenile

Marshland: A piece of land consisting of marshes, in which the water covers the ground for long periods of time

Toucans: A tropical American fruit-eating bird with a massive bill
Yacu-toro: A huge spectacular black-and-red cotinga bird with a strong, heavy bill
Surucua: A species of bird in the families native to South America
Parabellum: Refers to the
9×19mm Parabellum firearms cartridge for the Luger pistol
Menial: Unskilled or routine
Machete: A broad, heavy knife used as an implement or weapon
Stifled: Suffocate or choke
Chiquito: A Spanish word meaning 'tiny'
Hijito mio: A Spanish phrase meaning 'my son'
Mio: A Spanish word meaning 'mine'
Diminutives: A shortened form of a name
Garzas: Also called Heron, these are long-legged, long-necked, freshwater and coastal birds in the family Ardeidae
Pia pia: It translates from Spanish and is a phrase meaning 'daddy daddy'

Rokeya Sakhawat Hossain, India

(9 December 1880 — 9 December 1932)

Rokeya Sakhawat Hossain, also known as Begum Rokeya, was a Bengali feminist writer, thinker and political activist. She has been hailed as one of the most prominent voices for women's liberation in South Asia in the 20th century.

Begum Rokeya was born in an affluent Bengali Muslim family in the village of Pairaband, Rangpur, Bengal Presidency. Rokeya's elder brother, Ibrahim Saber, taught English and Bengali to Rokeya and her sister, Karimunnesa Khanam Chaudhurani, who later became a poet. Rokeya was married at the age of 18, to a 38-year-old Khan Bahadur Sakhawat Hossain, who encouraged her to pursue her literary dreams and suggested that she learn English and Bengali.

Throughout her literary career, Rokeya wrote about women's condition in Indian society and stressed the need to grant them equal social status to men. She also established the first school for Muslim girls in Bengal. Rokeya's writing style is inflected with logic, creativity and a dry sense of humour. Some of her most famous works include Matichur, Sultana's dream, Padmarag and Boligarto, among others.

Rokeya continued her mission to provide women with their rightful place in society, until her death in 1932 at the age of 52 due to heart complications. She is considered an important figure in Indian literary history, and her works showcase the vast scope of imagination that can be covered when women are allowed to express themselves to their fullest potential.

Sultana's Dream

One evening I was lounging in an easy chair in my bedroom and thinking lazily of the condition of Indian womanhood. I am not sure whether I dozed off or not. But, as far as I remember, I was wide awake. I saw the moonlit sky sparkling with thousands of diamond-like stars, very distinctly.

All on a sudden a lady stood before me; how she came in, I do not know. I took her for my friend, Sister Sara.

Sultana's Dream was originally published in The Indian Ladies' Magazine, Madras, 1905, in English.

'Good morning,' said Sister Sara. I smiled inwardly as I knew it was not morning, but starry night. However, I replied to her, saying, 'How do you do?'

'I am all right, thank you. Will you please come out and have a look at our garden?'

I looked again at the moon through the open window, and thought there was no harm in going out at that time. The men-servants outside were fast asleep just then, and I could have a pleasant walk with Sister Sara.

I used to have my walks with Sister Sara, when we were at Darjeeling. Many a time did we walk hand in hand and talk light-heartedly in the botanical gardens there. I fancied, Sister Sara had probably come to take me to some such garden and I readily accepted her offer and went out with her.

When walking I found to my surprise that it was a fine morning. The town was fully awake and the streets alive with bustling crowds. I was feeling very shy, thinking I was walking in the street in broad daylight, but there was not a single man visible.

Some of the passers-by made jokes at me. Though I could not understand their language, yet I felt sure they were joking. I asked my friend, 'What do they say?'

'The women say that you look very mannish.'

'Mannish?' said I, 'What do they mean by that?'

'They mean that you are shy and timid like men.'

'Shy and timid like men?' It was really a joke. I became very nervous, when I found that my companion was not Sister Sara, but a stranger. Oh, what a fool had I been to mistake this lady for my dear old friend, Sister Sara.

She felt my fingers tremble in her hand, as we were walking hand in hand.

'What is the matter, dear?' she said affectionately. 'I feel somewhat awkward,' I said in a rather apologizing tone, 'as being a purdahnishin woman I am not accustomed to walking about unveiled.'

'You need not be afraid of coming across a man here. This is Ladyland, free from sin and harm. Virtue herself reigns here.'

By and by I was enjoying the scenery. Really it was very grand. I mistook a patch of green grass for a velvet cushion. Feeling as if I were walking on a soft carpet, I looked down and found the path covered with moss and flowers.

'How nice it is,' said I.

'Do you like it?' asked Sister Sara. (I continued calling her 'Sister Sara,' and she kept calling me by my name).

'Yes, very much; but I do not like to tread on the tender and sweet flowers.'

'Never mind, dear Sultana; your treading will

not harm them; they are street flowers.'

'The whole place looks like a garden,' said I admiringly. 'You have arranged every plant so skillfully.'

'Your Calcutta could become a nicer garden than this if only your countrymen wanted to make it so.'

'They would think it useless to give so much attention to horticulture, while they have so many other things to do.'

'They could not find a better excuse,' said she with smile.

I became very curious to know where the men were. I met more than a hundred women while walking there, but not a single man.

'Where are the men?' I asked her.

'In their proper places, where they ought to be.'

'Pray let me know what you mean by "their proper places".'

'O, I see my mistake, you cannot know our customs, as you were never here before. We shut our men indoors.'

'Just as we are kept in the zenana?'

'Exactly so.'

'How funny,' I burst into a laugh. Sister Sara laughed too.

'But dear Sultana, how unfair it is to shut in the harmless women and let loose the men.'

'Why? It is not safe for us to come out of the

zenana, as we are naturally weak.'

'Yes, it is not safe so long as there are men about the streets, nor is it so when a wild animal enters a marketplace.'

'Of course not.'

'Suppose, some lunatics escape from the asylum and begin to do all sorts of mischief to men, horses and other creatures; in that case what will your countrymen do?'

'They will try to capture them and put them back into their asylum.'

'Thank you! And you do not think it wise to keep sane people inside an asylum and let loose the insane?'

'Of course not!' said I laughing lightly.

'As a matter of fact, in your country this very thing is done! Men, who do or at least are capable of doing no end of mischief, are let loose and the innocent women, shut up in the zenana! How can you trust those untrained men out of doors?'

'We have no hand or voice in the management of our social affairs. In India man is lord and master, he has taken to himself all powers and privileges and shut up the women in the zenana.'

'Why do you allow yourselves to be shut up?'

'Because it cannot be helped as they are stronger than women.'

'A lion is stronger than a man, but it does not enable him to dominate the human race. You have neglected the duty you owe to yourselves and you have lost your natural rights by shutting your eyes to your own interests.'

'But my dear Sister Sara, if we do everything by ourselves, what will the men do then?'

'They should not do anything, excuse me; they are fit for nothing. Only catch them and put them into the zenana.'

'But would it be very easy to catch and put them inside the four walls?' said I. 'And even if this were done, would all their business – political and commercial – also go with them into the zenana?'

Sister Sara made no reply. She only smiled sweetly. Perhaps she thought it useless to argue with one who was no better than a frog in a well.

By this time we reached Sister Sara's house. It was situated in a beautiful heart-shaped garden. It was a bungalow with a corrugated iron roof. It was cooler and nicer than any of our rich buildings. I cannot describe how neat and how nicely furnished and how tastefully decorated it was.

We sat side by side. She brought out of the parlour a piece of embroidery work and began putting on a fresh design.

'Do you know knitting and needle work?'

'Yes; we have nothing else to do in our zenana.'

'But we do not trust our zenana members with embroidery!' she said laughing, 'as a man has not patience enough to pass thread through a needlehole even!'

'Have you done all this work yourself?' I asked her pointing to the various pieces of embroidered teapoy cloths.

'Yes.'

'How can you find time to do all these? You have to do the office work as well? Have you not?'

'Yes. I do not stick to the laboratory all day long. I finish my work in two hours.'

'In two hours! How do you manage? In our land the officers, – magistrates, for instance – work seven hours daily.'

'I have seen some of them doing their work. Do you think they work all the seven hours?'

'Certainly they do!'

'No, dear Sultana, they do not. They dawdle away their time in smoking. Some smoke two or three choroots during the office time. They talk much about their work, but do little. Suppose one choroot takes half an hour to burn off, and a man smokes twelve choroots daily; then you see, he wastes six hours every day in sheer smoking.'

We talked on various subjects, and I learned that they were not subject to any kind of epidemic disease, nor did they suffer from mosquito bites as we do. I was very much astonished to hear that in Ladyland no one died in youth except by rare accident.

'Will you care to see our kitchen?' she asked me.

'With pleasure,' said I, and we went to see it. Of course the men had been asked to clear off when I was going there. The kitchen was situated in a beautiful vegetable garden. Every creeper, every tomato plant was itself an ornament. I found no smoke, nor any chimney either in the kitchen -- it was clean and bright; the windows were decorated with flower gardens. There was no sign of coal or fire.

'How do you cook?' I asked.

'With solar heat,' she said, at the same time showing me the pipe, through which passed the concentrated sunlight and heat. And she cooked something then and there to show me the process.

'How did you manage to gather and store up the sun-heat?' I asked her in amazement.

'Let me tell you a little of our past history then. Thirty years ago, when our present Queen was thirteen years old, she inherited the throne. She was Queen in name only, the Prime Minister really ruling the country.

'Our good Queen liked science very much. She circulated an order that all the women in her country should be educated. Accordingly a number of girls' schools were founded and supported by the government. Education was spread far and wide among women. And early marriage also was stopped. No woman was to be allowed to marry before she was twenty-one. I must tell you that, before this change we had been kept in strict purdah.'

'How the tables are turned,' I interposed with a laugh.

'But the seclusion is the same,' she said. 'In a few years we had separate universities, where no men were admitted.'

'In the capital, where our Queen lives, there are two universities. One of these invented a wonderful balloon, to which they attached a number of pipes. By means of this captive balloon which they managed to keep afloat above the cloud-land, they could draw as much water from the atmosphere as they pleased. As the water was incessantly being drawn by the university people no cloud gathered and the ingenious Lady Principal stopped rain and storms thereby.'

'Really! Now I understand why there is no mud here!' said I. But I could not understand how it was possible to accumulate water in the pipes. She explained to me how it was done, but I was unable to understand her, as my scientific knowledge was very limited. However, she went on, 'When the other university came to know of this, they became exceedingly jealous and tried to do something more extraordinary still. They invented an instrument by which they could collect as much sun-heat as they wanted. And they kept the heat stored up to be distributed among others as required.

'While the women were engaged in scientific research, the men of this country were busy increasing their military power. When they came to know that the female universities were able to draw water from the atmosphere and collect heat from the sun, they only laughed at the members of the universities and called the whole thing "a sentimental nightmare"!'

'Your achievements are very wonderful indeed! But tell me, how you managed to put the men of your country into the zenana. Did you entrap them first?'

'No.'

'It is not likely that they would surrender their free and open air life of their own accord and confine themselves within the four walls of the zenana! They must have been overpowered.'

'Yes, they have been!'

'By whom? By some lady-warriors, I suppose?'

'No, not by arms.'

'Yes, it cannot be so. Men's arms are stronger than women's. Then?'

'By brain.'

'Even their brains are bigger and heavier than women's. Are they not?'

'Yes, but what of that? An elephant also has got a bigger and heavier brain than a man has. Yet man can enchain elephants and employ them, according to their own wishes.'

'Well said, but tell me please, how it all actually

happened. I am dying to know it!'

'Women's brains are somewhat quicker than men's. Ten years ago, when the military officers called our scientific discoveries "a sentimental nightmare," some of the young ladies wanted to say something in reply to those remarks. But both the Lady Principals restrained them and said, they should reply not by word, but by deed, if ever they got the opportunity. And they had not long to wait for that opportunity.'

'How marvelous!' I heartily clapped my hands. 'And now the proud gentlemen are dreaming sentimental dreams themselves.'

'Soon afterwards certain persons came from a neighbouring country and took shelter in ours. They were in trouble having committed some political offense. The king who cared more for power than for good government asked our kind-hearted Queen to hand them over to his officers. She refused, as it was against her principle to turn out refugees. For this refusal the king declared war against our country.

'Our military officers sprang to their feet at once and marched out to meet the enemy. The enemy however, was too strong for them. Our soldiers fought bravely, no doubt. But in spite of all their bravery the foreign army advanced step by step to invade our country.

'Nearly all the men had gone out to fight; even

a boy of sixteen was not left home. Most of our warriors were killed, the rest driven back and the enemy came within twenty-five miles of the capital.

'A meeting of a number of wise ladies was held at the Queen's palace to advise as to what should be done to save the land. Some proposed to fight like soldiers; others objected and said that women were not trained to fight with swords and guns, nor were they accustomed to fighting with any weapons. A third party regretfully remarked that they were hopelessly weak of body.

'"If you cannot save your country for lack of physical strength," said the Queen, "try to do so by brain power."

'There was a dead silence for a few minutes. Her Royal Highness said again, "I must commit suicide if the land and my honour are lost."

'Then the Lady Principal of the second university (who had collected sun-heat), who had been silently thinking during the consultation, remarked that they were all but lost, and there was little hope left for them. There was, however, one plan which she would like to try, and this would be her first and last efforts; if she failed in this, there would be nothing left but to commit suicide. All present solemnly vowed that they would never allow themselves to be enslaved, no matter what happened.

'The Queen thanked them heartily, and asked

the Lady Principal to try her plan. The Lady Principal rose again and said, "before we go out the men must enter the zenanas. I make this prayer for the sake of purdah." "Yes, of course," replied Her Royal Highness.

'On the following day the Queen called upon all men to retire into zenanas for the sake of honour and liberty. Wounded and tired as they were, they took that order rather for a boon! They bowed low and entered the zenanas without uttering a single word of protest. They were sure that there was no hope for this country at all.

'Then the Lady Principal with her two thousand students marched to the battle field, and arriving there directed all the rays of the concentrated sunlight and heat towards the enemy.

'The heat and light were too much for them to bear. They all ran away panic-stricken, not knowing in their bewilderment how to counteract that scorching heat. When they fled away leaving their guns and other ammunitions of war, they were burnt down by means of the same sun-heat. Since then no one has tried to invade our country any more.'

'And since then your countrymen never tried to come out of the zenana?'

'Yes, they wanted to be free. Some of the police commissioners and district magistrates sent word to the Queen to the effect that the military officers certainly deserved to be imprisoned for their failure; but they never neglected their duty and therefore they should not be punished and they prayed to be restored to their respective offices.

'Her Royal Highness sent them a circular letter intimating to them that if their services should ever be needed they would be sent for, and that in the meanwhile they should remain where they were. Now that they are accustomed to the purdah system and have ceased to grumble at their seclusion, we call the system "Mardana" instead of "zenana".'

'But how do you manage,' I asked Sister Sara, 'to do without the police or magistrates in case of theft or murder?'

'Since the "Mardana" system has been established, there has been no more crime or sin; therefore we do not require a policeman to find out a culprit, nor do we want a magistrate to try a criminal case.'

'That is very good, indeed. I suppose if there was any dishonest person, you could very easily chastise her. As you gained a decisive victory without shedding a single drop of blood, you could drive off crime and criminals too without much difficulty!'

'Now, dear Sultana, will you sit here or come to my parlour?' she asked me.

'Your kitchen is not inferior to a queen's boudoir!' I replied with a pleasant smile, 'but we must leave it now; for the gentlemen may be cursing me for keeping them away from their duties in the kitchen so long.' We both laughed heartily.

'How my friends at home will be amused and amazed, when I go back and tell them that in the far-off Ladyland, ladies rule over the country and control all social matters, while gentlemen are kept in the Mardanas to mind babies, to cook and to do all sorts of domestic work; and that cooking is so easy a thing that it is simply a pleasure to cook!'

'Yes, tell them about all that you see here.'

'Please let me know, how you carry on land cultivation and how you plough the land and do other hard manual work.'

'Our fields are tilled by means of electricity, which supplies motive power for other hard work as well, and we employ it for our aerial conveyances too. We have no rail road nor any paved streets here.'

'Therefore neither street nor railway accidents occur here,' said I. 'Do not you ever suffer from want of rainwater?' I asked.

'Never since the "water balloon" has been set up. You see the big balloon and pipes attached thereto. By their aid we can draw as much rainwater as we require. Nor do we ever suffer from flood or thunderstorms. We are all very busy making nature yield as much as she can. We do not find time to quarrel with one another as we never sit idle. Our noble Queen is exceedingly fond of botany; it is her ambition to convert the whole country into one grand garden.'

'The idea is excellent. What is your chief food?'

'Fruits.'

'How do you keep your country cool in hot weather? We regard the rainfall in summer as a blessing from heaven.'

'When the heat becomes unbearable, we sprinkle the ground with plentiful showers drawn from the artificial fountains. And in cold weather we keep our room warm with sun-heat.'

She showed me her bathroom, the roof of which was removable. She could enjoy a shower bath whenever she liked, by simply removing the roof (which was like the lid of a box) and turning on the tap of the shower pipe.

'You are a lucky people!' ejaculated I. 'You know no want. What is your religion, may I ask?'

'Our religion is based on Love and Truth. It is our religious duty to love one another and to be absolutely truthful. If any person lies, she or he is....'

'Punished with death?'

'No, not with death. We do not take pleasure in killing a creature of God, especially a human being. The liar is asked to leave this land for good and never to come to it again.'

'Is an offender never forgiven?'

'Yes, if that person repents sincerely.'

'Are you not allowed to see any man, except your own relations?'

'No one except sacred relations.'

'Our circle of sacred relations is very limited; even first cousins are not sacred.'

'But ours is very large; a distant cousin is as sacred as a brother.'

'That is very good. I see purity itself reigns over your land. I should like to see the good Queen, who is so sagacious and far-sighted and who has made all these rules.'

'All right,' said Sister Sara.

Then she screwed a couple of seats onto a square piece of plank. To this plank she attached two smooth and well-polished balls. When I asked her what the balls were for, she said they were hydrogen balls and they were used to overcome the force of gravity. The balls were of different capacities to be used according to the different weights desired to be overcome. She then fastened to the air-car two wing-like blades, which, she said, were worked by electricity. After we were comfortably seated she touched a knob and the blades began to whirl, moving faster and faster every moment. At first we were raised to the height of about six or seven feet and then off we flew. And before I could realize that we had commenced moving, we reached the garden of the Queen.

My friend lowered the air-car by reversing the

action of the machine, and when the car touched the ground the machine was stopped and we got out.

I had seen from the air-car the Queen walking on a garden path with her little daughter (who was four years old) and her maids of honour.

'Halloo! You here!' cried the Queen addressing Sister Sara. I was introduced to Her Royal Highness and was received by her cordially without any ceremony.

I was very much delighted to make her acquaintance. In the course of the conversation I had with her, the Queen told me that she had no objection to permitting her subjects to trade with other countries. 'But,' she continued, 'no trade was possible with countries where the women were kept in the zenanas and so unable to come and trade with us. Men, we find, are rather of lower morals and so we do not like dealing with them. We do not covet other people's land, we do not fight for a piece of diamond though it may be a thousand-fold brighter than the Koh-i-Noor, nor do we grudge a ruler his Peacock Throne. We dive deep into the ocean of knowledge and try to find out the precious gems, which nature has kept in store for us. We enjoy nature's gifts as much as we can.'

After taking leave of the Queen, I visited the famous universities, and was shown some of their manufactories, laboratories and observatories.

After visiting the above places of interest we got again into the air-car, but as soon as it began moving, I somehow slipped down and the fall startled me out of my dream. And on opening my eyes, I found myself in my own bedroom still lounging in the easy-chair!

If you liked reading this story, you must also read:

Essence of the Lotus, The Secluded Women, Thirst, Murder of Delicia

---

GLOSSARY:

Zenana: the part of a house for the seclusion of women
Mardana: the part of a house for the seclusion of men
Sagacious: having or showing keen mental discernment and good judgement
Koh-i-Noor: one of the largest cut diamonds in the world